OPENELEVATOR

THE GOLDILOCKS TEAM

MASTER RETENTION AND HIRING

MINAL JOSHI JAECKLI

Copyright © 2025 by Minal Joshi Jaeckli
All Rights Reserved

ISBN: 979-8-89571-089-0 (paperback)

Dedication

To my clients. Your trust and courage to honestly uncover what lies below the surface speaks volumes about your leadership gravitas.

And to my beautiful family and friends.
I'm so lucky to have you!

Acknowledgment

Thank you to all the giants who have helped me see further. I endlessly appreciate the value of connection and collaboration as universal foundations for a high quality of life.

Praise for

The Goldilocks Team:
Master Retention and Hiring

———

"A bracing wake-up call to leaders mired in old ways of employee engagement and retention."

— Kirkus Reviews

"A comprehensive and refreshingly candid resource for every level of management."

— Self-Publishing Review

"Insightful, smart, and surprisingly entertaining, this is a must-read for leaders ready to build organizations where people feel purpose, not just pressure."

— Likely Story Blog

"It's not about hiring 'the best'—it's about hiring people who are right for you, your team, and your mission. That shift alone is revolutionary."

— Literary Titan

"A clear roadmap for leaders who want to hire and retain top talent for the long haul."

— Reedsy Discovery

"A book that every modern manager, team leader, or business executive must have on their shelf."

— Readers' Favorite

Contents

LET
PEOPLE
BE.

Preface

What is your formula for success?

For me, success comes down to a mix of hard work, ability, and a bit of luck, all underpinned by *a winning mindset*.

Since our strongest beliefs are the battle-tested ones, my success formula is based on a lifetime of experience. Not just with my career, but also with my family history.

Coming from three consecutive generations of immigrants, I've seen how these elements of success, hard work, ability, luck, all bolstered by mindset, shape how we recognize and seize opportunities. Specifically, my grandparents' journey from India to South Africa, my parents' journey from India to South Africa to Zambia and then to the US, as well as my own move from Zambia to the US and then to Switzerland, taught me the importance of these elements for success. As I'm sure you know, immigrating across continents brings both tremendous challenges and opportunities.

Like my upbringing around the globe, my career path has been anything but linear. I started my professional life as a chemist in the pharmaceutical industry before transitioning into various enriching and enjoyable corporate functions including project manager for a complex product-line in Silicon Valley and investor relations for the third largest wealth manager in Zurich, Switzerland. I loved these positions. I learned so much, had this wonderful pressure to deliver, and worked with great people. I could write a book on that phase alone. Then I became captivated by the topic of employee engagement. I was horrified when I realized how many people are unnecessarily unhappy at work, the toll it takes on their quality of life, and the impact it has on their organization's bottom-line. It's my mission to eliminate as much of that unhappiness as I can.

Over a decade ago, I founded OpenElevator to transform employee retention. I appreciate that I have successfully navigated completely new topics, thanks to my work ethic, analytical and communication skills, and, for sure, thanks to a lot of luck! This has allowed me to develop a system that has meaningfully improved organizations and people's lives.

Along the way, I have come to understand that the most successful teams, parallel to individual success, are (unsurprisingly) made up of hardworking, talented, lucky individuals, underpinned by something deeper. They're composed of people who connect with each other and work in environments that connect with their values.

Understanding the critical role of connection, I'm on a mission to not just talk about connection but show leaders how to identify who they connect with so they can build their best, top-performing teams. I look forward to showing you the value of connection in putting together your most successful team, to gain an unfair advantage in employee retention and hiring success. Ultimately, this book is a guide for mission-focused leaders looking to create winning teams that thrive.

Introduction

As a leader, it's easy for you to see yourself as the proud captain of a magnificent ship, all set for a critical voyage across the vast and unpredictable ocean. You've planned with great attention to detail for this crucial undertaking: your vessel has the highest-quality equipment, a well-thought-out route to get you to your destination, and an invaluable, talented crew. While you have the wisdom to know that some challenges are bound to show up, everything looks perfect for what you hope will be a smooth and successful journey ahead.

But once you leave the safety of the harbor and head into the open sea, you face an unexpected series of setbacks. Despite your best efforts and careful planning, progress is slow and storms loom on the horizon. Tension among the crew grows and you aren't certain you'll be able to complete your mission.

As problems mount, you ask yourself: *What's going on? What's wrong? What could I have planned better?*

You realize the on-going issue isn't with your sophisticated equipment or your carefully plotted route, you've been able to fine-tune your systems and strategy along the way. The problem lies with the crew you've chosen. They aren't necessarily all bad sailors, yet some are simply not delivering. And for those who are delivering, you worry issues among the crew are getting in the way of them getting things done. And what if your best crewmates jump ship? This voyage may not end in disaster, but it's not the smooth sailing you'd hoped for.

In the business world, you're captaining your own ship. You might have the latest technology, advanced strategies, and a vision that should take your organization to new heights. Yet despite these advantages, success seems elusive, perpetually just out of reach. The problem is often not with your systems or your strategy but your team's ability to execute that strategy, including their capacity to deliver to your standards, work easily with each other and their long-term commitment to your mission. You know very well issues with team members lead to frustration and setbacks.

But what if there was a better way? What if you could identify the best individuals before making hiring decisions? What if you could know who is happy, who is at risk of leaving and why in your existing team before they quit? What if you could know who works well together and where issues are brewing? What if you could know what to do so your top talent stays with you and is committed for the long-term? What if you could know all this, instead of having to guess?

Imagine how much easier it would be for you to achieve your goals if you had these answers.

The Goldilocks Team is here to make that possible. It is a powerful yet straightforward blueprint that will give you the insights you need to build and retain your best team for long-term success.

Why is Engagement Important?

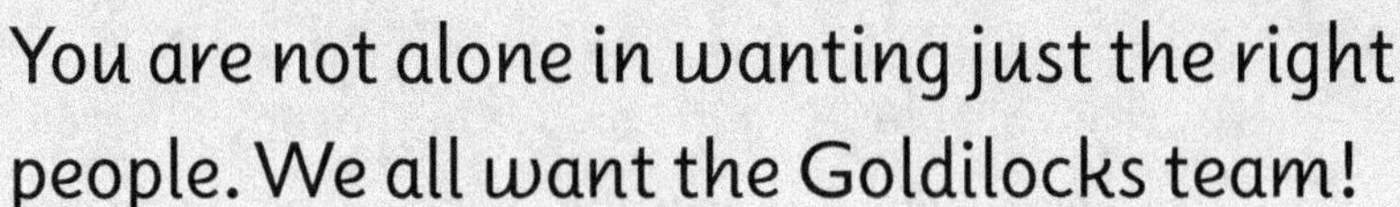

You are not alone in wanting just the right people. We all want the Goldilocks team!

How do you select your team? Who is right for you? As a leader, visionary, and builder, you know that a successful team isn't just made up of people with impressive resumes, it's so much more. Intuitively, we all agree we want the Goldilocks team, people that are *just right*.

Any expert will tell you how important hiring the right candidate is. Jim Collins, in his classic management book *Good to Great*, emphasizes the crucial value of getting the right people on the bus. Likewise, Jack Ma, the founder of Alibaba, advises to find the right people, not the best people.

While these pieces of advice sound simple enough, putting them into practice can be anything but easy. The real challenge is *tangibly* figuring out what "right" means, who the right people are and how to identify them amid a sea of candidates.

Ask a hundred people, or even just five, "What does the 'right' employee mean to you?" Be ready to get bombarded with all kinds of unmeasurable adjectives. "I like self-starters." "I look for people who have a positive attitude." Or my favorite answer to date: "You know, the 'right' employees have that je ne sais quoi!" Nice.

In addition to what makes for a "right" employee being elusive, there's an unrealistic expectation that "right" employees can adapt to any manager. Similarly, leaders are often expected to excel in managing team members under the assumption that the "right" leader can work effectively with anyone. These assumptions are not just unrealistic, they're completely wrong and lead to significant frustration.

In fact, there are no absolute "right" or "wrong" people; there is no litmus test for these labels. The truth is that, much like beauty being in the eye of the beholder, who is right and who is wrong for a position is subjective. (Actually, beauty is objectively measurable as we humans prefer symmetry, but that's off topic). One person's supportive boss can be another's micromanager and a colleague who seems eager to one person might come off as overzealous to another.

With no clear definition, much less measure, of "right," it's no wonder that despite your best efforts to assess if someone is right in an interview, some hires will not work well with you or with other team members. In fact, it's common for leaders to find themselves frustrated with the hiring process and struggling with team members who seemed right during the interview process and prove to be so wrong after onboarding. This inevitably leads to frustration, costs, and setbacks for the boss, the business, as well as leads to employee dissatisfaction, disengagement, and high turnover, all signs of a deeper issue: a hiring process that is outdated and ineffective.

Unfortunately, most organizations, not knowing there's a better way, continue to use unreliable hiring methods that haven't changed much over the last hundred years. While technology has made the process of sending and receiving applications faster, the heavy reliance on guesswork, as opposed to data, when assessing applicants for team fit remains unchanged. And most of us have fallen into the trap of hiring people who seem like a "good team fit," only to find out three weeks later that they have low standards, are consistently late, are sloppy, or are all around difficult to work with.

The old-school hiring approach often fails to address the core issue, finding the "right" fit for the manager, for the team, and for the environment. As a result, companies end up with employees leaving because they feel dissatisfied in their relationship with their boss and with their long-term prospects in the organization. And employers are left with the daunting task of repeating the costly hiring process, which can feel like playing the lottery with the odds just as long, hoping for better luck the next time around.

The Low Engagement Crisis

We all agree low engagement is not a fleeting issue to be taken lightly; unaddressed, the disruptions and costs pose significant long-term damage to a company's growth, innovation, overall competitiveness and bottom-line. Still, truly grasping the scope of the problem requires a deeper look at how persistent disengagement affects different aspects of your organization.

Disruption of Organizational Stability

Frequent turnover severely affects an organization's morale and degrades operational stability. Every departure and new hire creates a cycle of adjustment, disturbing team cooperation, productivity, and profitability. Like a line of dominos, when an employee departs, those who remain often face increased stress as they must take on the workload of their departed colleague and adjust to the new team dynamic. If you're familiar with the forming–storming–norming–performing model of group development, Bruce Tuckman's description of the inevitable phases a team goes through, then you may wonder, like I do: when does a team with high employee turnover ever start performing?

Even in the best case that knowledge isn't lost, the turmoil of a constantly revolving door makes it challenging to maintain a positive and productive work environment, leading to even more employees choosing to leave. You might have witnessed this predictable pattern: the more turnover you have, the more turnover you will have.

Innovation at a Standstill

When knowledge is lost, gone with unwanted leavers, innovation suffers. Innovation thrives on genuine commitment to delivering the best outcome, underpinned by deep organizational knowledge, seamlessly incorporating lessons learned and best practices from seasoned team members. High turnover undermines this, making it difficult for teams to focus on problem-solving and strategic initiatives.

No matter your industry, when employees are frequently changing, remaining team members spend a significant portion of their time onboarding new ones and integrating them into ongoing projects and processes to the best of their ability. This hinders innovation, slows down the implementation of new ideas, and increases overall risk.

Financial Costs of Turnover to Your Business

While low engagement leads to disruption and stalls innovation, the financial impact to the bottom-line reveals most clearly what this means for a business on an annual basis.

There is a mountain of data on the sheer scale of this problem of low engagement for the employer and employee, with more published daily. It is unfortunately a very hot topic for click bait, as many prey on the desperation of employers.

Gallup has been conducting its annual employee engagement survey for decades, consistently publishing low engagement rates ranging from mid-twenties to even mid-teens globally. As a leader, you know what an uphill battle it is to deliver quality for internal and external clients with a disengaged team. Disengagement makes delivering flawlessly and maintaining your credibility a constant struggle.

If you've ever been disengaged at your job, you can understand what a sad state of the world it is that four out of five employees hate going to work. Consider how much this erodes our quality of life. And it isn't just alarming; it's extremely costly. On a global economic level, these low engagement rates result in 7 trillion dollars of loss in productivity annually!

It's one thing to talk about the global economic impact of employee disengagement, but who can relate to a loss of trillions of dollars? So, closer to home, why is this important for you? What is the impact to your business?

One frequently measured consequence of low engagement is high employee turnover. Regardless of industry, the biggest cost for companies is its people. People-related costs can account for as much as 70% of total expenses. A significant portion of this is attributed to employee turnover costs, which are a substantial financial drain on organizations each year.

When we think of turnover costs, most of us immediately think of the direct costs associated with turnover, such as recruitment expenses, including job advertising, recruiter fees, and the time spent interviewing and onboarding new staff to replace the old.

However, in addition to direct costs, organizations also incur substantial indirect costs. The most obvious is the time required for new hires to reach productivity. Less obvious are the project costs due to valuable product or process knowledge lost with departing experts, as well as reputation costs that arise from disruptions in customer service when client-facing employees change frequently. Having been in client-facing positions throughout my career, I'm not sure there is anything more embarrassing, credibility-eroding, and ultimately customer-loyalty-destroying (and recurring-revenue-degrading) than clients sensing you have a toxic environment. It can cause them to worry about the impact your issues might have on them and drive them to mitigate their risk exposure by taking their business elsewhere. If you don't relate to what I'm talking about, you're lucky.

When considering the direct and indirect costs of employee turnover, Deloitte estimates that the total cost of losing a single employee can range from tens of thousands of dollars to 1.5 to 2 times their annual salary. The cost estimate encompasses the following three buckets:

1. the average 6 months of disengagement prior to resignation while an employee is on your payroll, phoning it in as they search for a new position,

2. the 6 months it takes to fill an open position, and

3. the additional 6 months needed for a new hire to become fully trained and productive.

For a rough back-of-the-envelope estimate of how much turnover is costing you, use this formula. Multiply your FTE, number of Full Time Employees, by your employee turnover rate. Then multiply the product by 1.5 times your average salary, from Deloitte's cost estimate range.

TURNOVER COST = FTE x Turnover Rate x Average Salary x 1.5

Or use the even simpler formula below, where 15,000 assumes a below average turnover of 10% (average is 13%) and average salary of $100,000 multiplied by 1.5, again from Deloitte's cost estimate range.

TURNOVER COST = FTE x $15,000

For a 100-person organization this results in an estimated cost of $1.5 million annually... Add to that the stress of having more departures than Chicago O'Hare, the reputational harm, and the impact turnover has on your targets.

Thankfully there is a better way. You can avoid these costs of low engagement with smarter employee retention and hiring strategies.

Engagement Pays Off Literally

Implementing strategies to increase employee engagement is not just about avoiding costs. There is significant upside to getting it right! According to Gallup, companies with highly engaged employees see:

- **2x retention**: Engaged employees stick around, which means you don't have to keep throwing time and money into recruiting, rehiring and retraining.

- **2x customer loyalty**: Engaged employees deliver more, so your clients get better service. This is how businesses get raving fans.

- **3x growth**: Companies with loyal employees grow faster, innovate more, and perform better. It's the magic of engagement!

- **30% higher productivity**: When people are engaged, they just work harder and smarter, leading to higher revenue. Plain and simple.

- **20% higher profitability**: Engaged employees innovate more, deliver better customer service, make more sales, and operate more efficiently, which means better margins and more profits for you and your business.

- **Nearly 150% higher earnings per share**: Companies with high employee engagement deliver significantly higher earnings per share vs. their competition.

I can't overstate the benefits of engagement and its ripple effects. Engaged employees lead to happy customers, which leads to a thriving business. It's a win-win-win!

What is Engagement?

———

Employee engagement is obviously extremely important. But what does it mean, exactly? Perhaps like me, you've worked for years without giving engagement a thought. Ironically, what got me interested in workplace engagement was my own disengagement.

After working across three industries on two continents and in about ten different mostly rewarding, if not totally fun, positions, from chemist in the pharmaceutical sector to product manager in the semiconductor industry to investor relations for a wealth manager, I joined Credit Suisse. I had a rich and diverse experience base to take on what sounded like a great opportunity. Beyond work, I was a lucky new mom, with the most wonderful husband. All was well. Even though I had joined the workforce over a decade ago, I had never said, much less thought about the phrase "Employee Engagement."

> "It is a truth universally acknowledged that when one part of your life starts going okay, another falls spectacularly to pieces."
>
> —Bridget Jones, Bridget Jones's Diary

At Credit Suisse it felt like the music stopped. Within a few weeks, I found myself completely disengaged.

While I'd had the usual career ups and downs, for the most part I had been very fortunate. I didn't fully grasp how fortunate until I joined Credit Suisse. As I often tell people, engagement isn't like a Bollywood movie, there's no dancing in fields of daisies when you're happy. It just feels normal, just like what you'd expect. However, when you're unhappy, dread Mondays, and feel a deep, soul-crushing aversion for your job, the difference becomes painfully clear.

Having worked in so many different environments, I tried to identify the throughline, the common thread among the positions that made them great (or at least fine). And what was missing now that was making me so unhappy? What was not working? What did I need to be happy?

I was horrified when I realized my disengagement at Credit Suisse wasn't an isolated issue but a systemic problem. I was struck by my colleagues' discontent. Every conversation revolved around the latest management upheavals, contained sarcastic comments about internal communications, and was evidence of everyone's overwhelming sense of frustration with their jobs, bosses, and the organization as a whole. My coworkers didn't just complain; people busied themselves, constantly networking to find another position to jump to, playing a desperate game of musical chairs. I wondered how any work got done. It was completely bizarre and nauseating to me. Unhappiness at work was not just an individual experience but a collective norm. Witnessing how they had normalized unhappiness at work was disturbing to me.

I felt like a spoiled brat for expecting more from work.

Was it that bad at Credit Suisse? Yes. Was I expecting too much from an employer, and from work, because of my own previous, rewarding work experiences? No.

It's striking how much our expectations and standards are shaped by our experiences and beliefs. In stark contrast to my previous positive experiences, I was now part of an environment where discontent was routine, and the pursuit of a fulfilling career was overshadowed by a prevailing sense of desperation and resignation. But I don't do desperation or resignation. I'm like a heat-seeking missile when it comes to problem solving; a dog that just can't let go of a bone (not always an enjoyable attribute for those around me). I needed a solution. So I set out to find one.

Of course you know, before solutions comes knowledge. Lucky for me, learning new things, new industries, new technologies, new functions, and new geographies, was the hallmark of my career. Instinctively, I set out to learn everything I could about what we need from work, what makes us happy at work, what drives engagement.

As I began to understand more about workplace happiness, I realized the depth of the problem. It wasn't just me, or The Credit Suisse Group. Employees and employers all over the world urgently need a different, better approach to talent management. This increasingly took hold and called me to develop a solution.

In the years that followed, I learned several critical lessons about talent management. Firstly, I understood that a toxic work environment can become an accepted norm if left unchecked. Knowing this has led me to focus on creating tools and strategies for companies to hire for engagement and build workplaces where satisfaction and contribution are prioritized from the start.

Like any first-order solution, addressing the root causes of disengagement is paramount. It is key to transforming both individual experiences and organizational cultures, powerfully impacting employee quality of life and company bottom line.

The Fundamentals of Engagement

How have I gotten so far without the fundamentals?

You know that the world is rich and fascinating, mind-blowingly abundant with things to learn and experience. With so many options, having a BSc in Chemistry and an MBA, in my formal education I have never had a class on what I need to be happy, in life or at work. Thankfully it's never too late to learn!

To understand happiness at work, I spent a lot of time reading. There is so much to be learned from the great works of Peter Drucker, the father of modern management, to the already mentioned books by the heroic Jim Collins, to Dave Logan's wonderful *Tribal Leadership*. With my doctorly handwriting, I made scrappy notes. The more I learned, the more I started to see the key pillars of job satisfaction. It was not an endless list of what we need from work. Rather, the following four key themes emerged: 1) safety & certainty, 2) contribution & purpose, 3) growth & significance and 4) connection & belonging.

	Maslow's Hierarch of Needs	Tony Robbins' 6 Human Needs	Ikigai "a reason for being"
Safety & Certainty	Safety	Certainty Variety	What you can be paid to for
Contribution & Purpose	Self-Actualization / Fulfillment	Contribution	What the world needs
Growth & Significance	Achievement / Esteem	Growth Significance	What you are good at
Connection & Belonging	Love / Belonging	Connection	What you love

Since I had done both molecular and financial modeling, I was versed in structured thinking. Developing an employee engagement model was easy. I was so excited, and remain in awe still, when I stumbled upon this quote from Gallup which sums up my model perfectly: "Employees are more likely to be engaged if their basic human needs are met." Amazing!

Our Basic Human Needs

Me (at 17 years old): "Isn't it weird how little original thought there is?"

Judy (my uber-confident friend): "I don't know about you, but I have original thoughts all the time."

Me: "That is also not an original thought."

While I certainly like to think that I'm original, an international woman of mystery, the consensus seems to be that I'm not. I'm driven by the same universal needs as everyone else. We have several frameworks for understanding these needs. You might be familiar with: Maslow's Hierarchy of Needs, Tony Robbins's 6 Basic Needs, Ikigai, or some other happiness framework. No matter the specific verbiage, they all include our need for: 1) safety & certainty, 2) contribution & purpose, 3) growth & significance and 4) connection & belonging.

Our Basic Human Needs at Work

Google conducted a study called Project Aristotle and confirmed the need for these exact attributes in the workplace, safety & certainty, contribution & purpose, growth & significance and connection &

belonging. In their quest to understand and optimize their workforce, they studied 180 teams, conducted 200+ interviews, and analyzed over 250 different team attributes. Here are the top attributes that successful teams share, ranked from fourth to first, with the first being the most important, and what they look and feel like at work, as well as the impact they have.

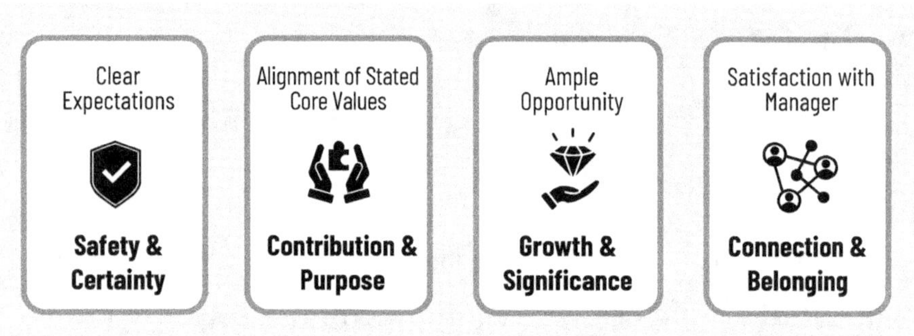

4th => Safety & Certainty. This shows up as clear expectations. When this need is not met, the looming uncertainty is frustrating at best, to anxiety-inducing such as in restructuring and layoff environments. Sadly, even after conducting such an extensive study with Project Aristotle, Google has still opted to do layoffs.

When this need is met, people have clear goals and roles, and get things done as agreed. This also shows up as a good sense of work/life balance as individuals feel that they can take time for other aspects of their lives. They have a healthy sense of control and feel secure regarding their standing in the organization

3rd => Contribution & Purpose. This shows up as alignment of stated core values. This is all about "walking the talk." When companies have glossy, polished mission and vision statements that are not lived, it is sarcasm-inducing and fosters cynicism towards management and the organization.

However, when there is alignment, people believe their work has purpose and impact. They feel they're working for the greater good. This fuels them to go the extra mile on a regular basis.

2nd => Growth & Significance. This shows up as having ample opportunity for advancement. Like Tony Robbins says, "in life, you're either growing or dying." Lack of opportunity is the #2 reason people leave their jobs.

When individuals have opportunities for growth, their work has personal significance, they feel recognized, and have a sense of progress. This fuels their commitment for the organization.

1st => Connection & Belonging. This shows up as satisfaction with the manager. This is THE #1 attribute that successful teams share. An employee's relationship with the manager is so important that their engagement can vary by as much as 70% from manager to manager in the same organization. When there is dissatisfaction with their manager, it's 80% of the time and the #1 reason people leave their jobs.

A good relationship with a boss gives individuals a sense of belonging and makes them feel safe to take risks and voice opinions. This is where ideas, innovation and creativity show up.

If you're already familiar with Maslow's framework, you will notice two things: 1) our basic need for survival is not included as a driver of employee engagement, since we don't depend on our employer for survival and 2) I've ranked the needs, not according to Maslow's hierarchy, but in terms of the impact they have on employee engagement *generally,* not for an individual specifically.

As individuals, we don't prioritize these needs the same. And, very importantly, we don't choose which needs are most important to us. While we all have a choice on how we behave to meet our needs, nature and nurture significantly determine our programming.

This plays out on the biochemical level. Our neural system's four feel-good "happy hormones," endorphins, serotonin, dopamine, and oxytocin, regulate our states. What triggers those hormones is out of our control. This reminds me of Arthur Schopenhauer's aphorism, "You can have what you want, but you can't want what you want."

For you as a leader, the take-home point is that these drivers of engagement are very deep seeded, not prioritized the same by everyone, not self-directed and not easily changeable.

What Engagement Looks Like

How can you tell if someone on your team is engaged?

While we all realize engagement is far more than people showing up to work, it can be hard (or even downright impossible) to recognize by just looking at your team members. It can be especially difficult to pinpoint who has one foot out the door. A lot of leaders I speak with are hard on themselves, scrutinizing which signs they missed, doing a postmortem after an unexpected, and painfully surprising, resignation.

By definition, engaged employees are emotionally connected to their organizations. Emotional connections are hard to see, but you know who consistently, and without any drama, goes the extra mile. Those are your engaged employees. They behave like stakeholders in your organization, delivering not just to the letter of the law but in the spirit of the law as well. You know you can pay people to do things, but you can't pay people to care. Engaged employees care.

I realize I have not answered the question, "What does engagement look like?" Well, that's the point. You will not be able to look at your team members and see it on their faces. On the other hand, you have felt someone's disengagement intensely when you've been on the receiving end of truly abhorrent service. So even though you might not see it, your customers will.

Now that we've talked about what drives engagement and how it impacts the way your team members show up in your organization, let's time travel to understand where we've come from, where we are and where we're going.

03

How has Engagement Evolved?

"In my day, we just got on with it."

-my dad, whenever he heard an excuse he didn't buy.

Our History of Engagement **The Current State of Engagement** **The Future of Engagement... Now!**

We understand that meeting basic human needs drives engagement, but why does there seem to be greater demand for meeting these needs now, more than ever before? Are the newer generations just a bunch of snowflakes? No, they're not.

The Engagement Evolution

There are two forces driving the demand for meeting our basic human needs at work: 1) what employers require from employees has changed and 2) what our culture requires from employers has changed.

How Employers' Requirements Have Changed

Let's zoom out and consider the history of work and how it has evolved – and continues to evolve.

Over thousands of years, there has been constant adaptation to changes worldwide based on resources, technologies, political systems, etc. Very interesting, but far beyond the scope I can cover here. In broad strokes what we see are shifts in demand, oscillating between: unskilled and skilled labor; generalist and specialized workforces; and more and less hierarchy.

If we were to time travel about 250 years back to the start of the Industrial Revolution, as factory workers where in demand, we would see an overwhelmingly rural population abandon the apprenticeship system and take jobs in cities. We would witness labor needs shift. There was increased demand for unskilled labor, increased specialization and more hierarchy compared to rural, mostly agricultural environments, where the masses previously worked.

Fast forward to today's developed nations where automation and offshoring are increasingly taking over repetitive jobs and what we have are more jobs than ever before in the service sector. These jobs in first world countries require less physical labor and demand skilled, specialized workers who bring creativity, innovation, and customer service. Employers no longer just need warm bodies, they need engaged, motivated, and committed people, who bring their hearts and minds to the workplace.

How Cultural Requirements Have Changed

As the work landscape has changed, what employees require from the workplace has changed, too, especially in the developed world. Not only because you get what you give, and greater demands from employers mean greater demands from employees, but also due to dramatic societal changes.

While our basic human needs have always been there, over time workers have started to expect these needs, once met by family, community, and faith, to now be met by the workplace. This transformation has been many years in the making. Already two hundred years ago, when people went to work in bleak factory towns, away from their extended, rural families, Henry David Thoreau famously wrote that "the mass of men lead lives of quiet desperation." People in those factories yearned for more.

Generally, as societies prosper, their perspective changes from working primarily to ensure safety and certainty to working to have growth and significance. Consider the TV show *Mad Men* set in thriving 1960s America. It wasn't just about safety and certainty anymore; it was about accumulating status, buying the new color TV and car, keeping up with the Joneses.

Sadly, bleak factory jobs still exist all around the world and that feeling of quiet desperation is still present there. It's also present among corporate jobs in the most polished looking companies. As Jim Collins echoed Thoreau a few decades ago when he wrote, "it is very difficult to have a meaningful life without meaningful work." Collins was talking about our fundamental need for more than a paycheck. Unfortunately, most companies have taken that to mean that they should have lofty, polished corporate mission and vision statements plastered on walls and websites. They aim to get buy-in on the buzz-word-filled rhetoric from all employees and even those just interviewing. The truth is: very few people are going to care about and share your corporate values and purpose. Everyone already has their own. The work needs to be authentically meaningful for each individual employee.

Over the years you might have felt the change to an ever-more purpose driven culture.

I remember, when I was growing up, adults asked, "what do you want to *be* when you grow up," focused on individual growth and significance. Today, young people are asked, "what are you going to *do* when you grow up?" focused on contribution and purpose.

There is talk of contribution and purpose everywhere. Oprah's "Live Your Best Life," the rise of TED Talks focused on purpose and meaning, and the growing conversations about mental health and wellbeing are just some examples of the change in what we demand from workplace culture.

It's no wonder every new generation is raising the bar on what they expect from their companies. In return, they're expected to deliver more of themselves. And who they're at work and what they do is the biggest part of their identity. And the demand on workplace culture will remain as quality of life continues to improve on a global scale, with individuals having more possibilities to bring their talents, more freedom to choose where they give their energy and consider more closely which company they align themselves with.

Before we get into what we can do to meet the demand of top talent so they want to spend their limited currency of time with us, let's talk about the basics of what not to do.

04

What Causes Disengagement?

> "Given A = B, and B = C, then A = C."
>
> – my 7th grade math textbook

Understanding that employees are engaged when their basic human needs are met, it just makes sense that actions that undermine safety & certainty, contribution & purpose, growth & significance and connection & belonging will damage engagement.

The Basics of What Not to Do

Unfortunately, most companies, while fully cognizant of the value of employee engagement, unwittingly do some or even all of the following:

Erode safety and certainty: with layoffs, layoffs and (did I mention?) layoffs. While you've most likely grown up with layoffs as a norm, up until the 1980s, mass reductions were primarily a last resort. They were either a reaction to a reversal in company-specific expectations, such as a competitor launching a market-share taking product, or a reaction to a reversal in the general economic outlook. They were not the blunt-force tool of choice to bolster share price quarter after quarter that they're today (which is not the same as smoothing earnings or cutting costs).

As a leader, it's important for you to understand that layoffs have massive engagement-destroying implications. The staff you lay off will move on, but those left behind will never trust you again. No matter the size of your internal communication budget, those remaining team members who witness their coworkers and friends being let go will always remember. They will smirk when you try to motivate them with lines like, "we're like a family." And those who can leave will at the very next opportunity.

I understand, "don't do layoffs" is very easy for me to write, when you may truly need to cut costs. I believe no one takes the decision to execute a layoff lightly. Yet, as layoffs are more common today, I think the consequences are considered less often. I have seen companies rush to calculate the cost savings from a 5% reduction in FTE (Full Time Employees) many times. Not once has one of those financial statements ever included the long-term costs of a disengaged workforce. In addition, if you examine results post-layoffs, you might be startled to know that for most companies, the cost savings from workforce reductions never materialize, while restructuring costs always do, as does the negative impact on engagement.

Another safety destroying practice is forced ranking of employees. If you're doing this, please stop. In case you don't know of this anxiety-inducing yet shockingly popular, archaic way of comparatively rating employees, consider yourself lucky. Here's how it works in a nutshell.

Managers are forced (*forced* is the key word here) to rank their team members on a scale (1-3 or 1-5) with a fixed percentage in each bucket. For example, let's say your company has implemented a 1-5 scale (with 1 labeled "poor performance" and 5 labeled "outstanding performance") and you're a team head with ten people reporting to you. At the end of the year, you must allocate your ten team members into these 5 ratings, so that for instance 1 person must be rated a 5, 2 are a 4, 3 are a 3, 2 are a 2 and 1 must be a 1.

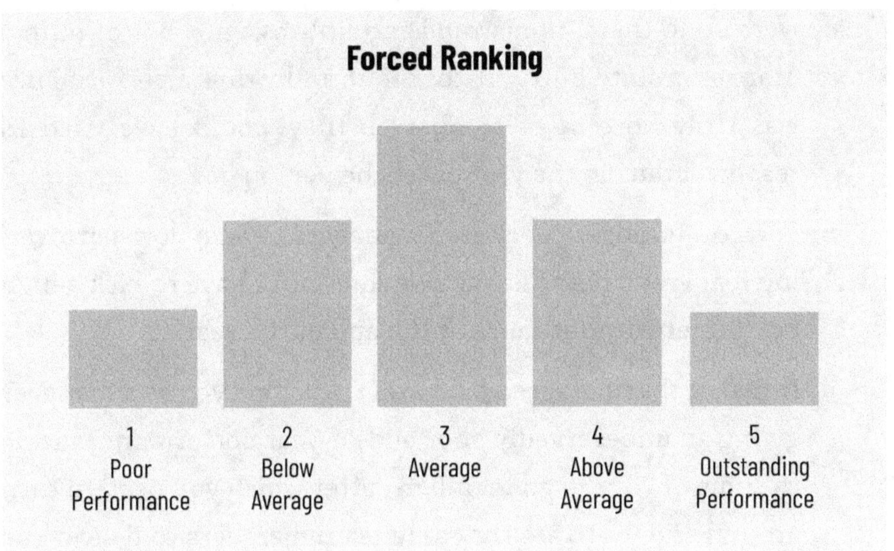

This method has proved to have no redeeming benefits, except for perhaps making the math for allocating bonuses easier. With a deeply negative impact on companies, I have no idea how this ranking method has been sold to so many sober, un-lobotomized organizations. Here are some of the consequences of this practice:

- It forces managers to rank productive team members negatively even when they have met expectations. Someone's got to be at the bottom. Imagine having to fail students who have completely grasped the material.

- Managers are left pitting team members against each other. This damages the manager-employee relationship and the individual's morale, especially since the rating can feel unfair to both manager and employee. Most managers will openly explain that their hands are tied; they must follow the senseless corporate directive. Many go as far as to say that if it were up to them, they would certainly assign a better rating. Managers state outright that if an individual's performance was truly bottom of the barrel, they would have tried to resolve it during the year or let the person go.

- Forced ranking incentivizes managers to keep low-performing team members just so that they don't have to kick a high performer without cause at the end of the year.

- It makes the manager's job harder. Imagine you as a manager giving an undeservedly poor end-of-year performance rating to some of your team members, after which you need to turn around and motivate the same team members to deliver the next year. How does that feel?

- Pitting team members again each other creates a competitive team environment instead of promoting collaboration. Forced ranking invites a mediocre stage 3 culture of "I'm great (and you're not)." Individuals focus on winning for themselves, hoard knowledge to ensure personal power and operate as lone warriors instead of as part of the team.

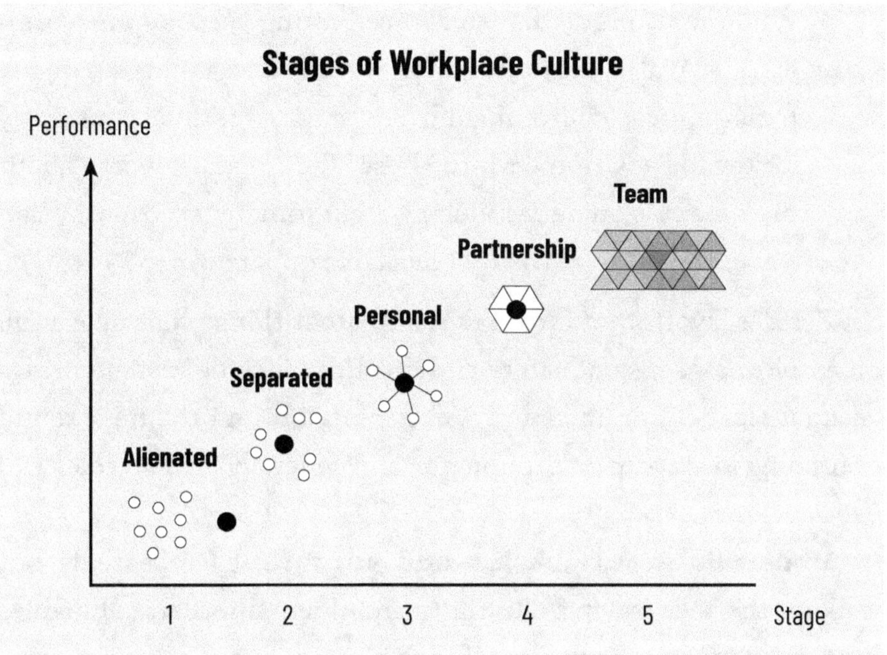

In *Tribal Leadership,* Dave Logan divides work culture into 5 stages summarized below.

1. Alienated: the individual feels alone and that "life sucks,"

2. Separated: the individual doesn't feel like a part of the team and that "my life sucks,"

3. Personal: the individual feels personally superior to team members and that "I'm great," implying the others are not,

4. Partnership: the individual feels proud to be a part of the team and that "we're great," and

5. Team: the individual feels part of a cause and that "life is great."

- While some argue that this forced rating keeps top performers, survival of the fittest, what it really does is create a highly toxic political environment where employees must constantly jockey for position with the boss. The constant worry about placement is anxiety-inducing and ultimately those who can leave, will do so at the first available opportunity.

Besides layoffs and forced ranking, other things that take a toll on employees' sense of safety and certainty include restructurings without clear communication, uncertainty around the next round of funding in startup environments, and generally unclear roles and expectations.

Undermine contribution and purpose: by repeatedly not walking the talk, saying one thing and doing another, companies hurt employee engagement. This is characteristic of larger organizations, many of which have indistinguishable, well-polished, consultant-drafted vision and mission statements. Company actions often render the well-intentioned words meaningless, or worse, they work in opposition to these carefully crafted statements. Worse still, and even more sarcasm-inducing, are the barrage of internal communication emails disseminated to spread a rhetoric that is simply not true.

Consider how often in your career you have seen messages claiming we're "all about quality," "customer focused," or "employees are our number 1 asset," followed by quite the opposite actions. Or how often you have received internal emails that outright insult your intelligence, such as the ones that thank senior leadership for their years of contribution and wish them well as they have decided to resign and go spend more time with their family. Let's hope someone has warned their family!

If you're in a leadership position able to decide, ask your internal communication team to take a break and see if anyone misses these messages. You will likely gain time and money to spend on better things.

The point is, trying to portray one set of values, which sound good, while living another, which are genuinely held, is difficult and fosters cynicism. In the long-term, this toxic cynicism makes the work feel worthless and destroys morale. Ultimately, this results in high turnover in an organization.

Crush growth and significance: many companies consistently favor recruiting external candidates before considering promoting from within. This external hero bias weakens engagement. So often, top decision-makers are blinded by shiny-object syndrome: swayed by an impressive former employer's name or elite school, only to bring on someone who also just puts their pants on one-leg at a time. Or, in the worst case, they bring on a brash, inexperienced outsider who seemed highly charismatic and had that extra dose of leadership mojo during the interview process, but who ultimately causes long-term damage to the organization.

At the core of long-term engagement, which is jargon-intensive, is the simple desire for leaders to have loyalty from their team, right? The thing is that loyalty goes both ways. If an organization is disloyal to its people, it shouldn't be a surprise when they're disloyal back.

Miss the boat on connection and belonging: this is the most important and yet the biggest failure of them all that leads to disengagement. As Brené Brown says so beautifully, "We're hardwired for connection." Connection is all about the relationship between two people. So, it's shocking to me that while we've come so far in so many areas, manager bashing is still completely acceptable. Just look at your LinkedIn feed and you will notice how much traction posts blaming bad bosses get. Even Gallup has published a book titled *It's the Manager.* Of course, they're spot on regarding the point that the manager has the most impact on an employee's engagement level. The failure is that it's NOT the Manager, but the *Relationship* with the Manager that's the issue.

To drive home my point, imagine how absurd it would sound if I said that marriages fail because "It's the Men." This blame game is not helpful nor accurate. Think about a time when you (or someone you know) were in a relationship that ended, and how you (or they) went on to be in successful relationships with other people, some without changing, much less improving in any way.

The two important points are: 1) it's all about the manager-employee relationship. And 2) like other relationships, as a leader, your management style resonates with some and not with others. Again, blaming one side, bad manager or bad employee, is not helpful nor accurate.

Now that we've talked about what not to do, from layoffs to forced ranking to unnecessary outside hires to blaming the manager, let's turn to how we set ourselves up for retention. What are the foundations of our retention strategies? Are we killin' it?

05

The Current State of Retention

How do we currently ensure retention? Let's look at who owns retention in our organizations, where the challenges show up, and which strategies we have in place to address these challenges.

Our History of Engagement	The Current State of Engagement	The Future of Engagement... Now!

The Clue: Who, Where and with Which Weapon is Killing Retention?

Remember the classic boardgame Clue? The object of the game is to solve Mr. Boddy's murder. Answer who, where and with which weapon he was killed. Well, we're going to play the game now to answer how we're killing retention. We're going to look at *who* owns the responsibility for driving employee engagement in an organization, *where* retention challenges arise and with *which* strategies we are aiming to retain employees.

The Big Misconception: "It's All About Corporate Culture"

The role of corporate culture is to employee engagement as vitamin water is to your health. I'm not saying it has no impact. But it's close to zero.

There is such a mass delusion regarding the role of corporate culture, and most of us know this on some level. For a long time, we've put the burden of employee engagement firmly on corporate culture, expecting it to ensure employee engagement with an invisible hand. It's easy to think that if a company can create the *right* culture, everything will fall into place. There is a glamorization that with the right messaging, the Internal Communication team, with emails, newsletters and mission statements, should be able to install a winning culture and create harmony. Like a great orchestra conductor.

Yet we all know corporate culture is not like a room scent that can just be defused. The reality is that while corporate culture is important, its impact on an employee's experience is overestimated and can be in stark contrast with the corporate image. Most people have experienced this firsthand. Below are some examples of perceived corporate culture versus an individual's lived experience.

- If you've changed departments within a company, you have likely witnessed that values lived in one part of the organization have little to do with those lived in another. For example, maybe you recall when Hewlett Packard introduced their "invent" campaign in 1999, as a way to return to its innovative roots? The goal was to rebrand externally as a forward-thinking company as well as reignite a passion for inventing within the organization. However, we can safely assume HP encouraged its R&D team to "invent" more than its accounting team.

- You may have felt firsthand a completely different vibe on one campus versus another. Just imagine the stark difference in values between the legitimate stockbroking business operated from the 18th and 19th floor of the Lipstick Building versus the large-scale fraud perpetrated by Bernie Madoff and a small group of employees on the 17th floor. It's mindboggling.

The Leadership Influence Paradox: It's Not All from The Head

Perhaps like me you've heard "the fish rots from the head," meaning if a company is struggling, the problem is likely the top management. Funny enough, it's not true in either case. Fish rot from the gut first. And while corporate leadership can absolutely set the tone for company culture, especially in terms of authentic values, ethics and compliance, real employee engagement happens on a personal level. Given that 1 out of 4 people don't even know the name of their CEO, it's understandable that an individual's boss, the person they interact with regularly, has far more influence on their job satisfaction than any speech or action from top management.

The reality is that, when it comes to engagement, an organization is only as strong as its individual links. In fact, Gallup's research shows that engagement can vary by up to 70% from manager to manager within the same organization. This point is so important; you will see that I will repeat it throughout the book.

The Misplaced Responsibility on HR: It's Not on Them

Would you blame the waiter for your poorly cooked meal or the chef for rude service?

It makes no sense that organizations defer to HR to improve employee engagement and increase employee retention when HR (unlike the direct manager) has little impact on a given employee's engagement level. How often have you worked in an organization and not even known the name of your HR person?

Even if your HR person has the best of intentions, there is little personal consequence for them if someone on your team leaves or stays. In fact, the bigger your organization the less impact any one departure will have on your HR team. Consider the following scenarios:

- What if your best salesperson leaves? It will likely hurt your bottom-line and your Head of Sales' targets and bonus. What is the impact on HR? None.

- What if your most senior engineer leaves? It will likely affect your product roadmap and your Head of Engineering's targets and bonus. Impact on HR? None.

As a leader, you know handing over responsibility to someone to achieve a result without understanding capability and aligning incentives is a recipe for failure. Therefore, if you're expecting your HR department to solve your high turnover problems, when they have neither the capability nor the incentive to deliver measurable results, you will be waiting a long, long time for results. Strangely, this is an open secret that so many leaders, especially at large corporates, don't seem to know. I'm sure part of the issue is a principal-agent problem. As soon as the topic of employee engagement comes up, so often CEOs and CFOs immediately leave the conversation to their HR folks. They assume their HR person knows best, has complete understanding of best practice, including the latest and greatest methods and tools available, and is totally willing to spend time on the topic where they have no personal upside if engagement and retention increase, but all the downside risk of making a bad call.

As it stands, managers have the biggest influence on their team member's engagement and are personally positioned to benefit most from the productivity of their team members. Therefore, for real impact, the responsibility for engagement and retention must be with the direct manager and not with HR departments.

Where Retention Challenges Arise

Me (at 25 years old): "I'm not a people person."

Susan (my sassy friend): "I was wondering when you were going to realize that!"

In my early 20s, I worked at a tech company in a product management role, where I drove the development of the next-generation product while ensuring support for the existing install base. I found myself *laterally* managing a diverse group of professionals: software, hardware, manufacturing, and tech support engineers, to name a few. Most of them were significantly more experienced and senior than I was. "Laterally" managing essentially means that your team members don't have to follow your directives, as you're not their boss and have no authority over them. To get things done, you need a solid set of influencing skills and a healthy dose of patience.

Over the decades, I've learned from working in various positions and with clients of all sizes and stages, from startups to multinational corporations, that, whether you *laterally* manage, inherit an existing team, personally hire each team member, or select a co-founder who you've known for years, challenges are bound to emerge, especially when the fit is not right. No matter how much authority you have, or think you have. The reality is that no one has full authority, only the power to influence. And there is no one-size-fits-all way to influence.

When we zoom out, the struggle for you as a team head comes down to the wonderfully positive and intensely negative impact team members can have on you, your goals, reputation, and results. Unlike in school when you alone primarily determine your grades. If you've worked with people on Earth, you've likely experienced at least one of the following disastrous working relationships:

Lack of Solid Capability: an individual simply lacks the skills necessary to deliver what's required. In our "fake it till you make it" culture, it can be tough to gauge an individual's true competence up front when so many present themselves as subject-matter experts. Unfortunately, an inability to perform the job is a definite dealbreaker.

Lack of Long-term Engagement: when an individual is not satisfied in their current role. You might sense their dissatisfaction, or they might directly express their desire for higher pay, greater responsibility or a different role. As a leader, you're either unaware of what you can do to ensure the person stays, or you're not in a position to accommodate the individual's requests. This feels like a no-win situation because you want and need engagement but simply don't know what to do or don't have the means to do what it takes to get it.

Lack of Smooth Collaboration: individuals who just prove "difficult" for you and your team to collaborate with. It can be endlessly frustrating when team members consistently fail to meet your standards for timeliness and quality, don't manage to keep you in the loop, struggle to grasp priorities, or don't communicate in a straightforward way. We all just want to avoid these types of people and (non-)working relationships.

While the pain of managing people can be intense, nothing stings quite like a surprise resignation.

Many clients turn to my company, OpenElevator, when they feel blindsided by yet another unforeseen resignation. They experience anxiety over the repercussions: increased workload for the remaining team, the potential risk to their goals, and damage to their reputation. They're frustrated, wondering who else is planning to leave and how they might get ahead of it. Engaging a recruiter yet again feels like playing the hiring lottery and more of the same.

Leaders experiencing a surprise resignation viscerally understand that finding someone capable of doing the job is just one part of the equation; knowing whether that person stays committed in the long-term and will mesh well with the team is an entirely different challenge. They know that unless capability, engagement and collaboration are all present there will be issues down the road. Up to this point they have relied on their instincts during the hiring process but have come to realize that it's exactly those instincts that have landed them in this situation.

Retention Strategy: Legacy & Trends & Guesswork, Oh My!

When it comes to the complexities of talent management, it often feels like a 'chicken or egg' problem: should you focus on retaining your current team members or on the hiring process? Most leaders instinctively first try to focus on retaining their current team for long-term engagement before diving into hiring new talent. It just makes sense since resources have already been invested on recruiting and training the current team. In my experience, no matter how formally or informally defined, every organization has a retention strategy. Unfortunately, their strategies are based on the following:

Legacy: Companies, including startups, implement retention strategies based on what they have always done or based on their experience at a previous employer. How could ABC Corp., with thousands of employees, not already have the best retention plan? How could the great Wizard not be wise!

Trends: In a rush to be like the cool kids, especially those in Silicon Valley, organizations adopt fads: colorful coffee areas, sushi Fridays, bring your dog to work. Search "retention strategies" online and you too can have the "26 Most Effective Employee Retention Strategies In 20YY" at your fingertips! Good luck with that.

Guesswork: Too often, companies rely on gut feelings when it comes to retention. If I had a dime for every time I've heard, "Oh, I know what my people want." It's like navigating a maze without a map, blindfolded! Meanwhile no one even packs for a vacation without checking the weather app. Then doesn't it just make sense that companies base important decisions regarding employee retention on information rather than guess?

Considering that our retention strategies are based on legacy, trends and guesswork, is it really a surprise that retention rates are not improving?

Now that we've looked at the misplaced ownership of employee retention on corporate culture, top management and HR and the flawed basis of our existing retention strategies, let's look at the state of hiring. No matter which side of the hiring process you've been on, I'm sure this will resonate with you.

06

The Current State of Hiring

> "Sometimes it feels like we've come so far just to realize we're where we've always been."
>
> – probably every entrepreneur at some point.

1-Click buying introduced by Amazon back in 2000 was revolutionary, whereas the 1-Click applying to jobs is more blasé than trailblazing. Maybe you've been on the receiving end of an application where you wondered if the person even read the job description. It's so annoying.

With so many technological advances and ever more recruiting tools, you might find it hard to believe when I say: not much has actually changed in our hiring process in a century. The traditional hiring model has always included job descriptions, interviews, offers, start dates and surprises. Not always good ones.

The criteria for hiring success, unsurprisingly the same as what is required for successful retention, have also remained the same over the years. Specifically, hiring success requires:

- Solid Capability
- Long-term Engagement
- Smooth Collaboration

Yet, our hiring practices overlook methodically assessing these critical factors, leading to loopholes in talent acquisition and talent management. Before we can talk about the way forward, it's important to first understand the full extent of issues in our current hiring process. By identifying the problems, we can better address the root causes and pave the way for more effective strategies.

Inflated Job Descriptions

Job descriptions are often idealistic wish lists, packed with every skill and experience that a company dreams of finding. Even worse, they frequently fail to reflect the true nature of the position and exaggerate career development prospects, leaving candidates startled, especially top university recruits, by the contrary reality of the work environment. While companies feel the pressure to compete for top talent, this misalignment of expectations from the start contributes significantly to the dramatic and costly turnover rates. The odds of a new hire still being with you in 18 months is about 50%, a coin toss! Unsurprisingly, the rates are even worse for hires recruited right out of college into new graduate programs.

The Resume Trap

It's hard not to judge a book by its cover, it's exactly the cover that gets our attention. And it's equally hard not to judge resumes at a glance. In fact, when recruiters vet applicants and present a curated set for review to the hiring manager, recruiters typically spend only 7 seconds on each resume. It's speed dating on paper. How disheartening for hopeful candidates who have poured so much time and effort into crafting the perfect resume.

While resumes are designed to be snapshots of a candidate's

potential, they often fall short in helping us identify the best talent. At this very first encounter, unconscious biases toward elite schools, high-flying companies, impressive titles, seemingly great achievements, or even font choices can lead us to overlook whether someone will truly excel in the role and integrate well with our team and organization.

Interview Or Inquisition?

If resumes test our bias-free decision-making skills, interviews challenge us even more.

As interviewers, we come armed with our best-practice list of top questions; it's not our first rodeo. We're aiming to hire for attitude and we're going to suss out the *right* one with our best questions. And, even if we're not looking for it, there's no shortage of unsolicited advice from millions of people on LinkedIn about what to look for when hiring.

Meanwhile, candidates are just as prepared; it's not their first rodeo either. They present a polished, rehearsed version of themselves that often doesn't reflect their everyday work style, values, or skills. And who can blame them? Traditional interviews are high-stakes games of "Say the Right Thing" ("oh yes, I want to be part of your dynamic environment that values innovation"), often feeling like an endless obstacle course for the applicant. We're so used to this process, we don't even think anything of it. Yet, imagine being on a first date where you had to feign interest while the other person went on and on about their values, vision and mission?

While most hiring processes today involve sophisticated scrutiny from multiple rounds of interviews, to skills and personality tests (some even include facial emotion recognition tools), the emphasis remains (as it has for the last hundred years at least) on dissecting the candidate. Far less attention is paid (certainly zero analytics) to what the candidate values or how well they will collaborate with the manager or team.

I call this the "Cinderella Hiring Model." Just like in the story, we know everything about Cinderella: her sad backstory, admirable work ethic, warm personality, and she can dance in glass slippers!

But what do we know about The Prince? Only that he's filling a role, looking for a wife. Sure, Cinderella and The Prince live happily ever after, but that's a fairy tale. In real life, unless everyone in an organization is as perfect as The Prince or has no personality at all, our current one-sided assessment methods won't improve hiring success or deliver exceptional team collaboration, no matter how many top interview questions we ask.

The Guesswork Guru

"I'm a great judge of character." It's a phrase I often hear. But if it were true and there were so many people with this sixth sense, our employee turnover rates, and even our divorce rates, would tell a different story. In today's information-rich environment, it's shocking how many hiring processes still rely on guesswork rather than data, especially considering the damaging impact of a bad hire. Resumes fail us. Interviews fail us. And despite their overconfidence, "guesswork gurus" fail us.

While gut feelings and personal impressions can be helpful, our unconscious overreliance on them introduces cognitive biases and undermines the effectiveness of our hiring processes.

How much do our unintentional biases inform our employment decisions? The wonderful story of the Boston Symphony's "blind orchestra auditions," introduced in the 1950s, comes to mind. In an effort to reduce gender bias in hiring, the orchestra held auditions behind curtains, allowing musicians to perform unseen. Initially, the results showed little difference in who was selected. Suspecting the sound of high heels might reveal musicians' gender, the selection committee asked everyone to remove their shoes before auditioning. This simple change from the truly brilliant selection committee led to a significant increase in the number of women accepted into the orchestra. Over time, other orchestras adopted this practice, with meaningful results. For instance, the New York Philharmonic went from having no female musicians for decades to achieving 35% female representation by the 1990s!

Here are some of the most common biases that influence us at hiring time:

The Halo Effect

One common pitfall in intuitive hiring is the halo effect, where an interviewer's overall impression of a candidate skews their judgment of specific traits. For instance, if a candidate presents themselves well in the initial part of the interview, this positive first impression can lead to an inflated perception of their skills and qualifications.

This effect is so pervasive that even physical attractiveness can influence evaluations of intelligence and competence. Studies show that interviewers often assume someone physically appealing is also more capable, regardless of their actual qualifications. In fact, researchers have found that tall people make significantly more in a lifetime. Our bias results in us overlooking crucial areas of a candidate's experience or skills that don't align with the positive halo.

Confirmation Bias

Confirmation bias complicates the hiring process by causing us to seek out information that confirms our initial impressions of a candidate while ignoring evidence to the contrary. For example, if we're initially impressed by where the candidate went to school, relate to their interests or share their background, we may unconsciously focus on their strengths and overlook potential weaknesses. This selective attention can easily cloud our judgment and lead to poor hiring decisions. Sadly, research has shown that interviewers unconsciously favor candidates ethnically or culturally similar to themselves.

Order Effects

Order effects describe how the sequence in which candidates are interviewed influences hiring. Interviewers tend to disproportionately remember the first or last candidates they met with, which can distort their overall judgment. Candidates are evaluated unequally based on when they were interviewed rather than their actual qualifications.

The Bias Blind Spot

The bias blind spot is a meta-bias where individuals believe they're less susceptible to biases than others. This phenomenon can prevent employers from recognizing their own biases and adjusting their decision-making processes accordingly. Research has shown that HR professionals generally perceive themselves as less biased than their peers (they're not), which leads to a continued overreliance on flawed judgment. Perhaps you have encountered such professionals and even believed they were less biased? Yet as you know none of us can read what is in another person's mind and in their heart. And worse, an assertion of impartiality is just as likely to be made by someone more biased as by someone less biased.

From favoring those we find attractive to those who reflect our background, and even to the impact of timing or how we're feeling that day, it's astonishing how much unconscious biases influence our decisions. For our discussion, identifying every single bias isn't important. What matters is recognizing how deeply biases affect our decision-making and the value of leveraging data-driven insights to enhance our hiring practices and free them of unconstructive partialities.

While gut feelings are not inherently flawed or bad, it's helpful to check them against objective criteria whenever possible. After all, our goal is to make the best hiring decisions. By acknowledging biases and implementing data-driven metrics, organizations can drive towards more effective hiring practices that reduce turnover and build stronger, more engaged teams. Imagine what more reliable hiring methods would mean for you and your team.

The 3-Pillars of Hiring Success

To sum up, let's go back to the three pillars of hiring and retention success discussed earlier:

- Solid Capability
- Long-term Engagement
- Smooth Collaboration

Evaluating a candidate's capability is often the easier part of the process, not easy, just easier. How you assess for this is so position-specific that I will not even attempt to give you a contrived formula. However, what is even more challenging to evaluate for an organization, inundated by applicants, and as testified by my clients across industries and functions, is determining if a candidate will remain engaged for the long-term and how well they will collaborate with team members.

This latter challenge is precisely what led me to create the OpenElevator platform. I wanted to go beyond guesswork, beyond abstract theory, beyond broken legacy methods, to find a way to measure long-term engagement and collaboration. I was intent on offering employers something truly reliable, pragmatic, and applicable.

Successful hiring and retention results from understanding, assessing, and ensuring there is a good fit for you and your employees. Specifically, by focusing on capability, long-term engagement, and ease of collaboration, you can build an engaged high-performing workforce.

Understanding the value of data, many organizations are already using tools to help them better identify, secure and retain their teams. In the next chapter, let's look at some of the most popular hiring and employee retention tools out there. Perhaps you're currently utilizing some of these yourself.

07

What We Measure Today

When I started my journey down the road of understanding and unlocking employee engagement, there were already plenty of established surveys, personality assessments and team building workshops. Despite all these tools, the disastrous state of employee satisfaction and the massive costs incurred by many organizations from unrelenting high employee turnover proved they clearly weren't working. What I came to discover was that these surveys, assessments and workshops simply don't work; they do nothing to address employee engagement. Let's look into what each delivers.

The Engagement Surveys

There are so many employee engagement survey vendors. A quick search will put more than 30 outfits at your fingertips. Tasked to find the right one? With an evolving landscape of new suppliers, as well as new feature sets introduced by existing suppliers, you have your work cut out for you. Good luck HR!

As an employer, what you need the survey to tell you is simply: who is happy, who is not, why, and what can you do about it.

Generally, here's what you get:

Average

Depending on the size of your team, the survey will deliver *averaged* results. As the vendors will explain, anonymity is the only way to get honest responses. If you were to know who was unhappy, you might use that information to conduct a witch-hunt, punishing dissatisfied employees, perhaps terminating them ("You can't quit, you're fired!"). So, no witch-hunt, but what can you do with averaged data?

Consider a mother with three kids. The school guidance counselor calls her in for a conference and informs her the children are, on average, doing poorly in school. What can she do with that not-very-helpful information? Now imagine the difference if the guidance counselor explains that while Lisa is on the honor roll and Maggie has mostly C's, Bart is failing math. Now Marge (that's the mom's name, by the way) can take action. She can help Bart with math or hire a math tutor (perhaps sparing him the weekly indignity of having to write a phrase on the chalkboard a hundred times).

It's not different with employee engagement. Averaged data is a small step above reading tealeaves. You need to know who is unhappy, why, and what you can do about it in order to take effective action.

Analytics

With most vendors, you will certainly get data-rich analytics updated perhaps as frequently as every week! The sheer amount of data is intriguing (also overwhelming). A ton of data, but information? Not so much. In addition, many of these tools keep your team needlessly occupied with giving each other kudos, badges and points.

The constant updating of metrics might feel helpful but it's as silly as tracking marital satisfaction with each interaction: +1, left me a sweet note; -1, burnt dinner. It's missing the forest from the trees. Engagement, whether it's your spouse's or your employees', is driven by deep-rooted, core needs, for safety & certainty, contribution & purpose, growth & significance and connection & belonging. These are not changing week to week no matter how many badges you give out. Organizations that steer clear of those peddling real-time pulse checks are really doing themselves a favor.

Annualize

In my experience, the key thing these vendors deliver is an annual bill, unless you prefer to pay monthly. Companies get sucked into measuring results, like NPS (Net Promoter Score) year-on-year, quarter-on-quarter, as well as departments and locations and any other comparison that can eke out a positive story. But what does it change? For the rare company that stops the incessant evaluations and looks up, they find that, after considerable outlays of time and money, their employee turnover hasn't improved one bit.

The Personality Assessments

When I was hired as an SCA (Strategic Capability Acquisition, I'm not making that up) for a technology conglomerate looking to bring on top talent as part of their succession planning, I went through the usual prolonged hiring process. In addition to multiple rounds of interviews, I had a full day of psychological evaluations, including tests and interviews with a PhD. Some weeks after my assessment, I received a copy of the multiple-page report, which of course was a fun read.

You've probably taken at least one of these popular tests, since most companies use some type of personality assessment in their hiring process.

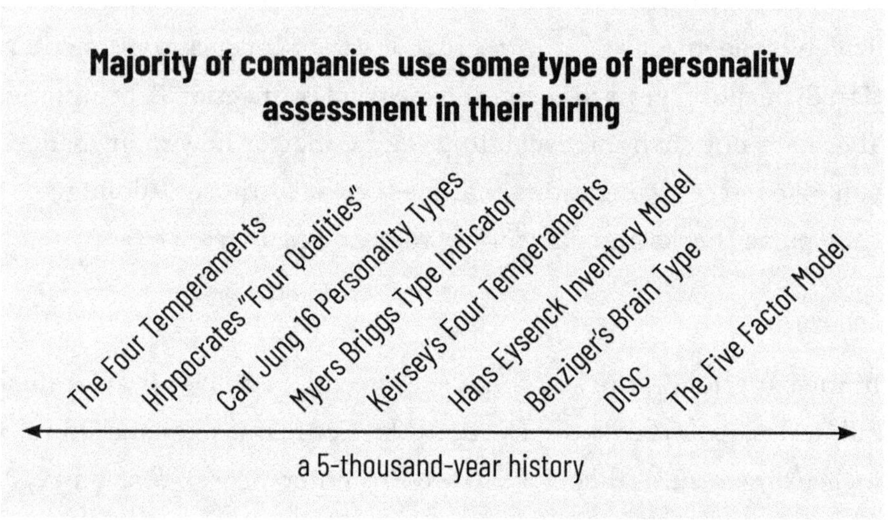

Over the years for various positions, I've done many more of these tests. I'm an ENFJ according to Myers Briggs, high DI (very red and yellow) per DISC, a Wolf/Warrior according to Relationship Archetype, and a Leo based on my birthday.

Does knowing all that give you important information about me? Does knowing someone's labels on any or all these tests help you make hiring decisions? Does it tell you who will work best with you and your team? Does it predict who is going to quit a week before a crucial deadline and throw your entire division into chaos? No. No, it does not.

On top of using personality tests during the hiring process, many organizations utilize them to give managers insight into their team members. Unfortunately, too often I have witnessed insights from one of these assessments being used to label and "fix" an employee.

I've had people share experiences like a boss commenting, "See your DISC profile? I told you—you're not assertive enough. I want to see you be more assertive in the next meetings."

Consider the fact that less than 10% of people stick to New Year's resolutions; we rarely keep deeply felt commitments we've made to ourselves to change. We certainly don't change for our parents, or partners, or our children. Then how realistic is it that we will change for our employer? No one wants (or needs) a boss to fix them. No one is looking to be Corporate Barbie or Company Ken, dressed up to look and act a certain way. Giving feedback on a team member's work is worlds different from trying to "improve" their personality. Let people be.

In addition to the fact that no one wants to be "fixed," if (like most of my clients) you have massive professional and personal goals and already have a lot on your agenda, you probably have little time for or interest in playing the Rubik's Cube equivalent of "will my team and I work well with ENFJ?" Just imagine how much easier it would be to know how well a specific candidate will collaborate with you and your team. And all without a psychology degree.

Team-Building Workshops

Along with engagement surveys and personality assessments, team-building workshops are a staple, especially in bigger organizations. While I've had a lot of fun with colleagues at these offsite events that last anywhere from a couple of hours to a full week, calling them "team building" promises far more than they can deliver. Maybe "at-work-sabbatical" would be a more fitting name. Well, whatever we call it, they do allow team members to get to know one another better, or meet employees from other divisions. But how do they impact your team members, your work and your organization when you're back at the office?

Let's face it, if you dread interacting with a difficult colleague, spending a day doing trust falls won't make them any easier to work with. Nor will hours of "I-statement" exercises make that unreliable coworker any more dependable.

Imagine how many workshop leaders, management consultants and politicians would go out of business if they were paid based on their positive long-term or even short-term impact.

| Our History of Engagement | The Current State of Engagement | The Future of Engagement... Now! |

What's Missing? What Do We Need?

While survey tools, personality assessment and team-building workshops may have their place, they're not practical tools for leaders looking to grow their business. Swimming in vast, non-actionable and potentially irrelevant data on your workforce is more than a distraction; it's a waste of time and money. Comparing year-on-year metrics of various departments to mete out rewards doesn't meaningfully improve the bottom-line of your business. Knowing the label one more personality test assigns someone tells you nothing of how well they will work with you and your team. And enjoyable though they may be, team-building workshops do nothing to change dysfunctional workplace dynamics.

What will benefit leaders are pragmatic, actionable, results-focused solutions that ensure smooth collaboration and long-term engagement.

As we close the chapter, it's clear that the issues we've discussed regarding the need to understand long-term engagement and collaboration potential aren't just obstacles, they're opportunities for transformative change. In the next chapter, we'll transition from frustration to innovation and demonstrate how data-driven decisions make for the best ultimate solutions, addressing disengagement, fulfilling basic human needs, and overcoming retention and hiring issues.

08

How Can You Engage Your Team?

Engagement requires capturing
hearts and minds.

By now you know the four drivers of engagement: safety & certainty, contribution & purpose, growth & significance and connection & belonging. The good news is that most companies, including yours, already have tools to address three: safety & certainty, contribution & purpose and growth & significance. These tools include your goal setting process, your mission and vision statements, and your annual review process. But the tools are not enough; to implement them effectively we have to understand their value in driving employee engagement.

Implement Existing Processes

To improve your team members' sense of safety & certainty, we have goal-setting processes for tracking milestones and KPIs (Key Performance Indicators) and for creating clear expectations. This sounds so basic, but even very senior people express frustration when what is expected of them is a moving target. When we set clear expectations, not only are we more likely to get what we want, we build credibility on both sides.

Regarding contribution & purpose, while you have a corporate vision & mission statement, as leaders, it's far more powerful if you can dig deep and uncover the values most important in your area. Perhaps it's increasing efficiency or building relationships with the best suppliers. Take Philip Morris's previous values statement, for example, "Defending the right to personal freedom of choice." Far from glossy words, their stated purpose was authentic to their business ethos.

For growth & significance, there is the annual review process, which is a time to review past performance as well as define a growth path for each person on your team. Of course there is a limit to the growth you can offer, and sometimes, it is hard for managers to see their team members move on. But in the long run, nothing good comes from holding someone back. The need for growth is natural.

In working with managers, frequently the issue is that there is a gap between having access to well-defined tools and how a team head puts them into practice. Meaning it's like the differences in fitness results between 1) knowing we should move more, 2) having a gym membership, 3) going regularly, and 4) carrying out a workout routine tailored to our goals. My aim is to show you where the gaps are between knowing what you should do and getting it done and to give you concrete steps to close the gap doing the right things regularly to achieve your goals.

Now, I want to underscore that my aim is not to add hours of things for you to do to engage your team. I hate when I go to an expert such as a fitness coach, just to be overwhelmed by their recommendations. I'm willing to do a lot, but working out (and counting my macros) is not the focus of my life; I can't (and don't want to) prioritize fitness at the level my coach does. In that vein, all recommendations here are geared towards delivering managers easily implementable results and prioritizing strategies that are low-hanging fruit. Well, not just any low-hanging fruit, the optimum low-hanging fruit.

Implement Best Practice Methods

You might be familiar with Samin Nosrat's Salt, Fat, Acid, Heat as the four basic factors that determine how good your food will taste. Yet we know that most people don't say "I enjoy salt," "I love fat," or "I want more acid." They say things like "I have a sweet tooth," "I love pastries," or "I add hot sauce to everything." Similarly, employees don't say they prioritize safety, contribution, growth, connection and so on. Most people don't even know which of the four core values they prioritize. What they're more likely to say and focus on is how it shows up in the workplace. Meaning, they are likely to voice that they want reasonable job security, a meaningful job, advancement opportunities and a good relationship with their boss.

The table below illustrates the four core needs and some examples of how they show up in the workplace.

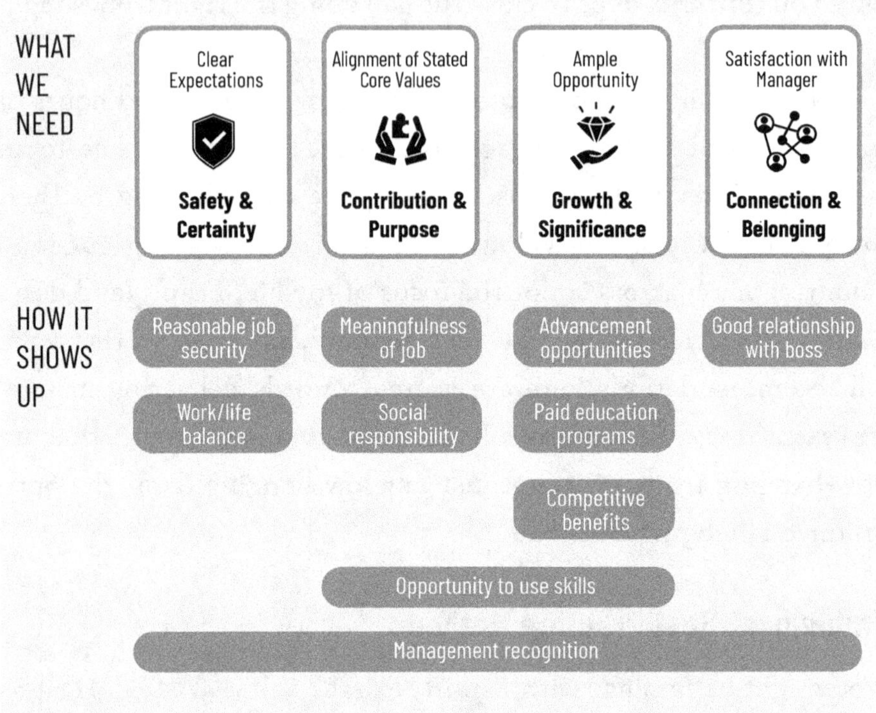

Not only do individuals prioritize these needs differently, but they also vary in cost and ease of delivery for a manager. See the table below which illustrates this for a large corporation.

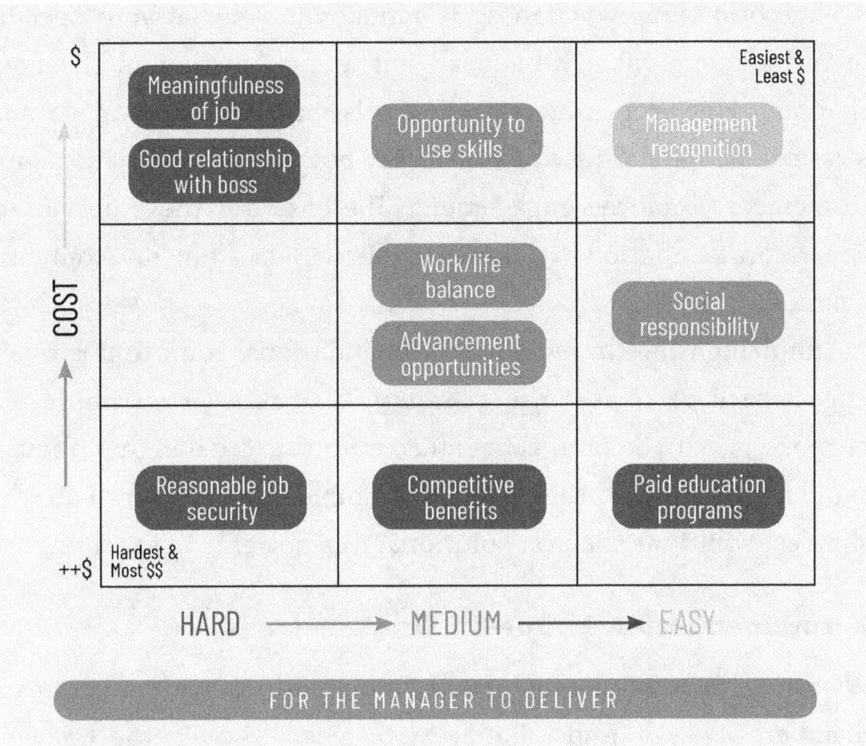

Note the following:

- **Reasonable job security** can be very hard and expensive, frequently not in a manager's control. Consider for example, when there is uncertainty and cost pressure on an organization from the macro-economic environment.

- Delivering **meaning** is almost impossible. Even though it's not costly, if employees feel that what they do is meaningless there is almost nothing a manager can do to change this feeling and install a new one.

- For a manager, at any level in an organization, delivering **management recognition** is the easiest and least costly. It requires no additional budget or approval in any organization.

The best thing you can do is actually know what your specific team members value, which we will discuss further in the next chapters. However, understanding this matrix of easy to do and least costly, here are two painless yet powerful recommendations to increase employee engagement. The basis for these best practice recommendations is the vast client data from my company OpenElevator.

Implementing these two recommendations, you can positively impact each person's sense of safety & certainty, contribution & purpose, growth & significance and connection & belonging. They're simple; you may find them even too simple. Yet, how often are the simplest solutions the best solutions? The power is in the doing.

Recommendation 1: One-To-One Meetings

When & Who: Schedule recurring meetings with each team member. My team and I like every 6 weeks; 4 weeks can be overwhelming depending on your team size and workload, and 8 weeks might let too much time pass between check-ins to have an impact. Consistency is key.

Why: These meetings increase safety and certainty by giving you an opportunity to proactively address issues before they escalate and manage your and your team member's expectations. They also reinforce contribution, purpose & significance by creating a space where you can recognize individual performance. And they impact growth by allowing you to uncover and define mid-to-long-term plans and recalibrate for any changes. And these one-to-one meetings help you simply connect.

What: We recommend a three-part agenda for these meetings as detailed below. Certainly, there is nothing magical about a specific question, the point is to help guide a productive conversation and deliver results for you and your team members.

Three-part Meeting Agenda Framework:

1. Reflect on the recent past since last meeting

    - How have things gone since our last conversation?

    - What are the highlights of your month so far?

    - What could have gone or been better in the last weeks?

    - Give feedback on where things could have gone or been better.

    - Acknowledge things that the team member got done and/or handled particularly well.

2. Plan for the next weeks

    - What will make the next month successful for you?

    - What kind of support do you need?

    - What would you like to do differently?

    - Announcements: this can include milestones, anniversaries, job openings, training opportunities & resources, such as local internal workshops, and recommendations for books, podcasts, or even apps you think would be helpful for them to know for their job.

3. Understand long term alignment (on a biannual basis)

    - How would you like your position to evolve in the next few years?

    - What can you do to make that happen?

- How do your goals align with department or company goals?

- Communicate your vision for your team, where you see alignment, and how you can support their goals, for growth, increased work/life balance, etc.

Recommendation 2: "Connect" Emails

When & Who: Send a regularly recurring "connect" email to your team, cc'ing your direct boss and other key stakeholders for greater impact. We recommend aiming to send about every 6 weeks, as with one-to-one meetings, every 4 weeks can be overwhelming, and every 8 weeks can be too infrequent to have an impact. Our clients find it helpful to use the last message sent as a template in their draft mailbox and update it with highlights more or less weekly. The key again is consistency.

Why: These emails let you share management insights on how your business is evolving, increasing safety. They can be a platform to tie individual members' work to the big picture, at team-level and/or department-level, and publicly recognize your team members with a broader audience. They can be a great tool to reinforce contribution, purpose & significance. And these emails can help position your team members for future opportunities with key stakeholders, tangibly and positively affecting growth.

What: We recommend a three-part connect email as detailed below. Clearly you might not always have content for a particular section; the outline is only meant to make this easy for you to carry out and benefit from.

Three-part Connect Email Framework:

1. Employee focused content

   - Recent wins: acknowledge team members for things they've done well recently. For example, a last-minute request someone handled particularly well.

   - Announcements: this can include milestones (completed or coming up), anniversaries, job openings, training opportunities and resources (such as local internal workshops).

2. Client focused content

   - Scope update: give status of existing deliverables, divided by the business area or client you serve, including any product- or process-related changes. Share information on any additions to your scope of responsibilities.

     Here you can also recognize team members instrumental in handling stakeholders' and/or clients' new topics or changes.

   - Client perspective: share your experience with or feedback from stakeholders, including internal and/or external clients. This is so meaningful for team members.

3. Company focused content

   - Company news: share organizational and operational updates, relevant industry or economic news (for example, an anticipated regulatory change), and upcoming events. Be sure to acknowledge the person on your team responsible for ensuring your offering reflects the newest updates.

- Policy or corporate changes: share any changes relevant for your team as long as they don't cause personal stress. For example, leadership changes, milestones achieved or a new holiday schedule. Things that might cause stress should be communicated in person, such as organizational restructuring that directly impacts team members. Announcing something like this via email is simply bad form.

My first clients were entrepreneurs at startups, open to my equally new and innovative data driven approach. As you can imagine, entrepreneurs, hustling like crazy to build their businesses, have few processes in place. So they were very grateful to have practical tools to engage their teams. What surprised me, and still surprises me at times, is getting that same grateful reaction from clients working in large multinational organizations with thousands of employees. We take for granted that big established organizations have superior processes. But this is simply not the case. Consider the companies you've worked for and how different, how well put together, they seemed before you started working there.

Our three-part meeting framework is designed to help clients gain clarity on where individual team members stand, address issues before they spiral, connect with coworkers on a human level, even via video calls. I never get tired of clients consistently and proudly reporting back how sending out the connect emails raised their leadership gravitas in their organization. And this positive impact is felt on both fronts, by their team members and by their senior leaders. Team members appreciate and respect the manager for delivering insights. And they beam with gratitude, yes, beam with gratitude, whenever they're acknowledged in these emails.

Senior leaders on these emails also praise managers for their leadership, impressed by the message bridging team tasks and projects to the bigger picture. Over time, my clients are promoted and given greater responsibilities.

Managers don't go to manager school; you learn on the job. Instead of forcing you to figure everything out by trial and error, simple practical tools can really make the difference - whatever your organization's size. I've seen this with clients over and over. It just makes sense that if you implement the two practices above, regularly communicate through one-to-one meetings and the connect emails, you will already be far ahead of most managers. After all, isn't communication one of the hallmarks of any relationship, be it marriage, friendship, or work?

Want a bigger edge? Keep reading.

09

Know Values Alignment

Imagine you have invited friends over for dinner. What you will serve depends on two things:

1. what your guests enjoy, based on their allergies, dietary preferences, palate, etc. and

2. what you can make, based on your cooking skills, budget, time, etc.

Knowing these two things is the start to defining and ultimately delivering a satisfying experience for you and your guests. After all, knowledge is great, but *applied* knowledge is power.

Leverage Insights to Upgrade Engagement

When it comes to a successful engagement and retention strategy, it's no different from your dinner party. Knowing what your employees value and what you can offer is the key. Specifically, here are two things most companies fail to do that will improve your employee engagement:

1. Base your retention strategy on what your employees value versus going on (and on) about your corporate values as others do and

2. Base your retention strategy on knowledge and data, rather than legacy, trends and guesswork like everyone else.

While we understand the four drivers of employee engagement, the myths, explicit or implied by Maslow's and Anthony Robbins and every other happiness framework, are 1) that there is a ranked order of what we value, 2) that everyone's ranking is the same and 3) that what we value does not change.

The fact is everyone priorities safety & certainty, contribution & purpose, growth & significance, and connection & belonging differently. One team member may need safety and connection far more than contribution, while another might feel the opposite. Some employees will have one or more needs fulfilled by other areas of their life, such as their family, community, etc., and won't look to the workplace to meet those needs.

And our needs change as major life events occur. Here are some examples you may have witnessed:

- Someone has a child, elderly parents to care for, or goes back to school, increasing their need for work/life balance.

- A colleague scarred by a recent layoff or a startup employee constantly worrying about the next round of funding will have a greater need for safety than they did before these experiences.

- After reporting to a manager they hate, an employee will give far more weight to working for someone they like. It's stunning how most of us don't realize how important a good relationship with our boss is until we've experienced the agony of a difficult working relationship. You've probably experienced that yourself.

To increase your team engagement, you have to know, based on data not guesswork, what each of your colleagues values. Then you can develop a winning engagement and retention strategy. You will quickly realize that this bespoke approach, you being engaged and taking care to deliver what your team members prioritize, is very much worth it. After all, engagement is a two-way street.

To understand your team members' priorities, you can develop a method in-house or leverage our platform, designed to do exactly that. Yes, no more guesswork!

Our system requires less than five minutes to deliver Values Alignment Data. You get a detailed report and a debriefing session. Leveraging this data will give you answers to the following critical questions:

1. What does each team member value?

2. What are the most important values across the team?

3. Who is least satisfied and therefore at highest risk of quitting?

4. What can you do to engage and retain those who are least satisfied, considering your specific business environment?

5. Which current incentives and business practices are a waste of time and money?

For any given team, from scrappy startups to multinationals to non-profits, what the data reveals is truly fascinating. With these insights in hand, our clients immediately move from assuming to knowing what specific team members value and what actions to prioritize. Once they see the data, they can't unsee it. With guidance tailored to your specific team, the right moves become obvious.

Having good data is transformative. Which is why after every debriefing where a leader first sees the data, they ask "Can I use this in hiring?" Of course you can. Why speculate when you can be certain.

Long term engagement depends not just on understanding what your existing team members value; you must discern what your potential employees value, too. There is no point in bringing on someone who will be disappointed, then disengaged, then (in all likelihood) departing, leaving you to restart the expensive and draining hiring and training process yet again.

What I Have Learned from The Data

We cannot assume from industry or company size, that we will know the answers to the questions above on what a team values. It's easy to think that bankers want growth, nonprofit workers want contribution. Wrong. Each team is unique and will answer our five-minute survey questions differently.

Another surprise: not everyone prizes growth! It's almost a fact ingrained in our collective unconsciousness, that people want to get ahead. Looking at the dataset, you see that this is simply not true. It's also not the case that Gen-whatever is more ambitious than other generations. People of all ages, at various stages in life, with evolving circumstances, have differing needs. Many give growth less weight than other, more pressing, values.

My biggest takeaway from many years of crunching numbers is that crunching numbers is the way to go. Without data, it's a stab in the dark as to what's going on below a team's surface. As one client put it, "it felt like *we switched on a light* and discovered what was hidden."

Shifting to Data-Driven Leadership

So far we have discussed how to affect three of the four drivers of long-term engagement (safety & certainty, contribution & purpose and growth & significance) with tools most companies already have. We emphasized that leaders gain an edge by not only addressing these needs generally, but by getting to know, with data versus guesswork, exactly which of these needs their team members hold dear. This allows managers to craft and implement a customized, powerful retention strategy that will measurably reduce employee turnover.

Ultimately, we all have the same goal. Whether you're leveraging data from our platform or another source, we want leaders and organizations to save time, money and frustration by creating a better work environment. It's a win-win for employers and employees.

So you have a choice to make. Are you the type of leader who resists the unknown in favor of sticking with the familiar, or are you prepared to try something new and base your opinion on the results. In the words of the poet Robert Frost, I invite you to take the road "less traveled by" and experience for yourself the power of data-driven retention strategies.

10

Know Interpersonal Alignment

Connection is THE prerequisite for team success.

You probably noticed in the last chapter that when we covered the tools most companies already have to address engagement, those methods only tackled three of our four top values: safety & certainty, contribution & purpose and growth & significance. What about connection? It's the most important driver of employee engagement. Connection is so important that if you get it right, the others take care of themselves. Truly, the value of connection in the workplace cannot be overstated.

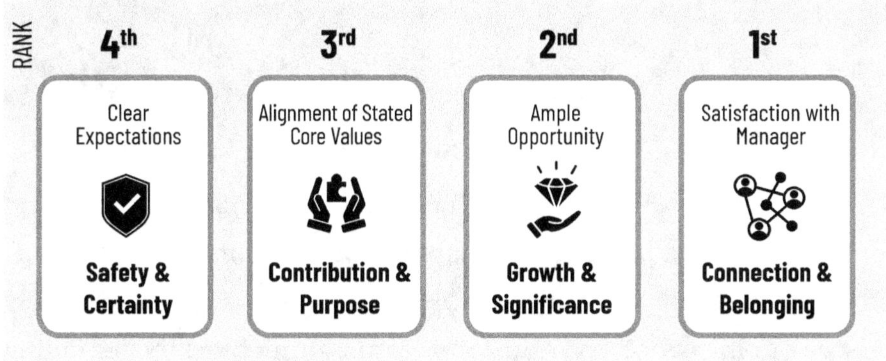

Get THE Biggest Unfair Advantage

We're hardwired for connection; our very survival depends on it. **Connection** is a prerequisite for **safety**, the foundation for **contribution**, and has a profound impact on **growth**. Connection is the number one driver of employee engagement. I remind you that an employee's relationship with their direct boss is SO important that engagement can vary by up to 70% from manager to manager in the same organization. And connection based on *alignment of specific attributes* naturally fuels collaboration! It's practically magic.

What are these *specific attributes*, you might be wondering. Don't worry, I will share that shortly. First, let's look at how connection impacts your end business goal, your bottom line.

The Steps from Connection to Bottom-Line Success

Let's start with the bottom line. Most people are pragmatic and understand that our goal in our organizations is to have positive bottom-line impact.

To ensure positive bottom-line impact, organizations focus on optimizing three pillars: sustainability, profitability and growth. A business that fails to be sustainable, profitable or to grow will likely not be a going concern for the long-term... think Blockbuster failing to be sustainable, Webvan failing to be profitable and Toys R Us failing to grow.

The levers to bolster sustainability, profitability and growth are innovation, creativity and customer service... think Amazon Web Services! At the heart of each success (and failure) is innovation, creativity and customer service (or the lack thereof), be it in terms of product, service or process.

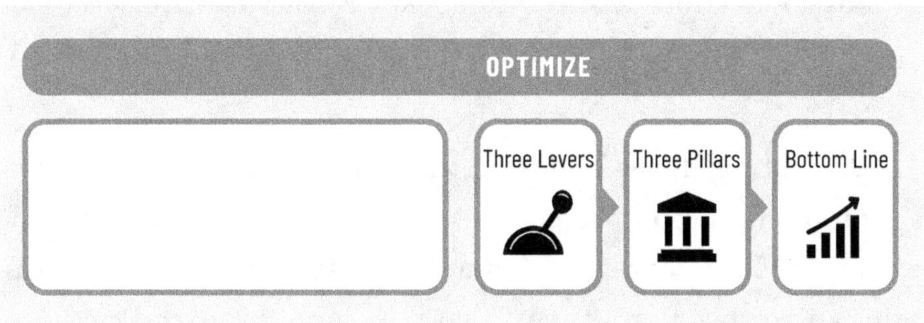

So, the question is "what is needed to improve innovation, creativity and customer service?"

Diversity.

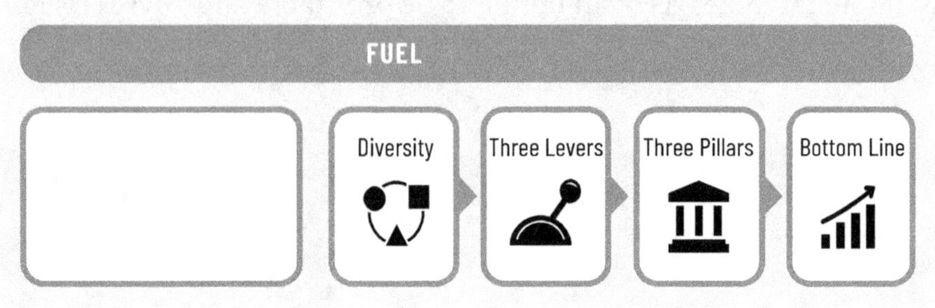

While diversity seems altruistic, and has unfortunately become very politicized, it's not just nice to have. Diversity feeds innovation, creativity and customer service. Wrongly, most people think of diversity as only an assortment of phenotypes, observable (or what they consider observable) differences. Yet it is so much more.

> **"As far as genetics is concerned, race does not exist."**
> —Adam Rutherford, A Brief History of Everyone Who Ever Lived: The Stories in Our Genes

Diversity includes non-observable traits such as experiences, education, ideas and perspectives. The table below lists just some examples. These observable and non-observable differences can bring an organization richness that fuels innovation, creativity and customer service.

Diversity
Observable & Non-observable

Physical Ability	Gender	Religion
Skills	Age	Value System
Talents	Sexual Identity	Political Views
Education	Sexual Orientation	Ethics
Languages	Family Status	Culture
Work Experience	Learning Style	Ethnicity
Life Experience	Work Style	Family History
Demographics	Thinking Style	Wealth
Nationality	Ideas	Social Status
Race	Beliefs	Heritage
Skin Color	Perspective	
Physical Attributes	Tastes	

Consider for instance, how much easier it is for team members with different perspectives, in a globally positioned organization, to understand, address and serve the needs of a diverse client base. Imagine the insights required on cultural diversity in the following examples.

- Variations in McDonald's Menus

   You might be more Michelin Star than golden arches, still you know the undeniable venerability of the McDonald's brand worldwide. One aspect underpinning their success across borders is their balance between offering continuity and localization. While they understand that most people go to McDonalds's, at home and abroad, for consistency in price, quality, and experience, it makes a lot of business sense, as McDonald's says, that it "adapts [its] menu to reflect different tastes and local traditions." Imagine the diverse local knowledge they must employ to do this as successfully as they have.

- Financial Advisors Offering Faith-Based Investing

  While risk appetite dominates most investment management courses, financial advisors and institutions grasp the importance of accommodating clients' preferences. This includes the demand for religious-based investment such as Biblically Responsible Investing following Christian principals, Shariah-compliant investing following Islamic law, and Jewish-oriented investment strategies that consider that faith's commandments and mitzvot. We can appreciate the depth of know-how required to be able to offer any of these investment vehicles in an authentic and credible way.

Pulling on this thread a bit more, we know that diversity *by itself* is not enough to fuel innovation, creativity and customer service. To quote the Harvard Business Review, "Diversity without *inclusion* is useless." Meaning, token minority representation on your team, board or website is not enough, or even the point. The impetus is in the genuine inclusion of diversity. Such as in the McDonald's and Financial Services examples, the successful outcome is due to the actual inclusion of a team's diverse knowledge.

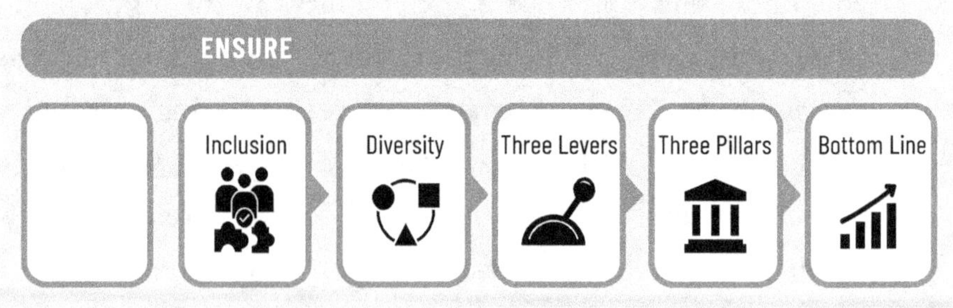

So, how do you achieve inclusion? When do you really *include* someone in your decision-making? Most people include those they're connected to. I have been very lucky throughout my career to have strong connections with experts whom I could consult on a range of topics and include in my decision-making.

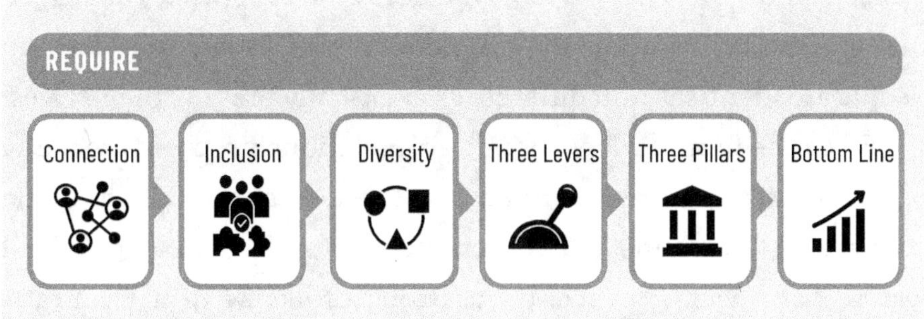

Think about the various decisions you make daily. Who do you include in your decision-making? Doesn't it come down to people you're connected to and, from your experience, trust to give credible, constructive input? You certainly aren't going to reach out to people you don't know or don't trust. Connection is the prerequisite for inclusion.

What is Connection?

Before we go any further, let's ask, "What is connection?"

Fundamentally, human connection is sparked when two people interact with one another, and each, to some extent, is heard, seen, understood and appreciated. Intuitively, we all grasp that there is a spectrum of human connection ranging from being casually acquainted with someone to knowing them fully, from your brief encounter with a standoffish barista to your relationship with your lifelong best friend. Incidentally, I believe this connection is limited by how honest and accepting people are regarding themselves; someone else can only know you as well you know yourself.

The first spark of connection, by default, is based on similarities. While it makes all who value diversity cringe, intuitively we connect, engage and trust people more who look and act like us. Without tools, how people look and act is the best proxy for assessing connection. Naturally the story does not end there, since no two people are identical, and differences eventually present themselves.

From the first spark to a long-term relationship, there are many opportunities to increase or decrease trust, to strengthen or erode connection. Over time, our actions increase or decrease trust which lead to a stronger or weaker connection. It's like we're all river rafting solo; the view is changing, the current is changing, the risks are changing. We don't know what opportunities to increase or decrease connection meeting each other will bring.

Connection at Work

Consider for a moment your closest friends. Like most people, there are probably some friends you can imagine working with easily and others not at all, which doesn't stop you from being friends.

While both personal and professional connections change as trust changes, there are two significant differences:

1. **Impact**: Your friends' behavior normally has no impact on your income, standing, results, and goals in your professional life. While your team members' actions impact your work directly, from your credibility with internal and external clients to your financial situation. In contrast, you turn to your friends for your emotional well-being, not (hopefully) your co-workers.

2. **Attributes**: You connect with people in your personal life on a breadth of attributes: shared interests, experiences, preferences, beliefs. But when it comes to work, connection is based on a very specific set of attributes. Not only are these attributes specific, but they're also subjective, including standards of quality, timeliness, structure, etc. People connect well with those who have similar preferences and fail to connect with those who don't. We will discuss the attributes more fully in a bit.

    Interestingly, personal and professional connections come down to how someone makes us feel. Colleagues who don't deliver in line with our standards, make us feel our credibility is at risk.

    As an aside, I would be remiss (and in trouble with my therapist friends) if I didn't add that no one can really "make us feel" anything. How we feel is a reflection on us, not the other person. Yet, considering the multitude of feelings that arise in a day, the best we can do is balance between being self-reflective and getting things done.

    Colleagues who "make us feel" that our credibility is at risk are just a long-term no-go.

The Impact of Connection

Fear is a bad advisor. Yet fear of how our co-workers will impact our work drives behavior. This fear weakens an organization. An organization, like a chain, is as weak or only as strong as the individual links between managers and employees.

Specifically, when the manager-employee link is weak:

- Employees worry about the security of their position, deliver the bare minimum, keep their heads down, and bide their time until they secure a job elsewhere. The environment feels political and toxic, and high employee turnover is inevitable. When these employees leave their position, instead of making an internal move, they're far more likely to leave the organization, never to return. That's how intensely employee's experience their relationship with the manager.

- Managers anguish over what might not get done and when they will need to step in to fight a fire. This insecurity leads them to micromanage to ensure deliverables are submitted on time and with sufficient quality. Managers, concerned about short-term outcomes, are left with little time and energy for long-term thinking.

When the manager-employee link is solid:

- Employees feel safe being their authentic self and empowered to bring their ideas to the table. A strong manager-employee relationship fosters innovation and creativity. Individuals not only worry less about their position, but they also feel the organization supports their growth. And they have a sense of contribution and purpose delivering for the team (yes, the two-person manager-employee team). Workers go the extra mile on a regular basis, without any drama. And, even when they leave an organization, these individuals keep in contact with the former manager.

- Managers feel safe to delegate. The relationship fuels progress as both team leader and member collaborate to deliver their best for each other and the organization. You see these teams improve products and processes, always with a long-term perspective, ultimately benefiting internal and external clients. Every so often, you will even see that when these leaders, especially top executives, join new organizations, their trusted team goes with them.

The departure of a top executive and their team can certainly alarm senior leaders. Those same executives are advised to take note if they hire a top manager, an external hero, and this person brings not one person from their former address.

While the manager-employee relationship is the number one driver of employee engagement, employee-employee relationships powerfully impact collaboration as well. The effect is not as pronounced but it is consequential. You can probably relate to this:

- When these relationships are weak, coworkers are frustrated, have a hard time moving things forward, avoid interacting with each other and can even sabotage each other and the organization. Unfortunately, to some extent, we have all experienced these difficult working relationships.

- When these relationships are solid, coworkers collaborate smoothly. Since pain is more noteworthy than pleasure, most of us overlook effortless collaboration. I mean, of course things are getting done... why wouldn't they be? Looking back, you can clearly name the people you worked with easily. Maybe, like me, you're very grateful for them.

The Attributes of Connection at Work

When I passed Bonnie, our procurement manager, by chance in the hallway, I asked casually, "Hey, what's the status of that part we've ordered?" She matter-of-factly replied, "Oh, since you didn't follow up with me, I thought you didn't want it anymore."

I was shocked.

Did Bonnie seriously expect me to ask multiple times to prove I really needed something? If there is an alternate universe, I'm still standing in that same spot, shivering in horror, 25 years later!

Moments like these, when I totally don't understand the way another person works, make me jealous of the amazing octopus. Octopuses are proof that intelligence evolved completely independently more than once, and I for one envy (the probably wrong belief) that they're antisocial. Just imagine how much easier life would be if we were alone and didn't have all those difficult people to deal with. Alas, we're human.

Have you ever spent time thinking about what makes some people easy to work with and others so very difficult?

Before I thought of creating a model to help employers and employees select their best teams that collaborate smoothly, I spent hours pondering this very question to uncover the answer.

Here's the answer: how well you work with another person depends on the overlap of a specific set of attributes. These attributes are subjective, based solely on what you consider appropriate ways to think, feel and act. We all believe our way of thinking is best, and the farther someone is from our "right" way of thinking, feeling, and acting, the more intolerable we find them.

Here's a scenario you can probably relate to.

At the end of a meeting, a person asks, "When can I expect you to get this to me?" Their colleague answers, "Next Tuesday."

What do you expect will happen? What is appropriate and reasonable? How do you feel about the following scenarios:

1. Colleague delivers by next Tuesday as agreed.

2. Colleague responds by end of Monday, with a heads up that more days are needed to complete the task.

3. Colleague delivers several days late, with no prior heads up, much less an acknowledgement, excuse or apology that the task is completed late.

4. Colleague delivers after two weeks have passed and only after failing to answer several follow up messages inquiring about the status.

5. Colleague doesn't deliver at all, even after follow up messages inquiring about the status have been sent.

Now, we know nothing about the nature of the meeting and can imagine various circumstances where each response is perfectly appropriate and reasonable (scenario 5, the colleague died).

The point is not to define which is correct, the point is to see that coworkers respond in various ways all day long. Your ability to collaborate with, or tolerate, people at either end of the 1 to 5 scale is based totally on you.

Although I'm a fun girl at dinner parties, I have a military-minded working style. So, for me, a coworker who consistently falls into categories 3, 4, or 5 is a total no-go. While for my editor Lorin, it might be perfectly fine.

Whatever works for you isn't right or wrong, it's just what you can tolerate. Though my way *is* best.

Zooming out, the folks who share your perspective on a few key attributes are the ones with whom you will work best. Including:

- they share and deliver in-line with your standards, versus other people's lax or unachievable demands

- they keep you in the loop, versus inundate you with too many details or leave out key information

- they share your priorities, versus others who don't

- they're as candid as you are, neither too sensitive, incapable of handling truths, nor tactless, even offensive at times

- they're straightforward versus hard for you to read

When two people are at odds on several of these attributes, a breakdown is on its way. Misalignment of attributes creates an atmosphere of mistrust; easygoing collaboration and joint success become impossible. Coworkers lacking shared attributes will find working together difficult and frustrating in the long-term.

On the other hand, when there is reasonable alignment of these very specific attributes, smooth, successful collaboration follows. Each positive interaction reinforces trust, belonging and respect, and working together to solve problems becomes second nature. As a leader, it is absolutely game-changing to have people on your team that you can rely on, even if you're not dancing in a field of daisies.

This value of attribute alignment also plays out at the team level. You might have teams that, despite having members who are individually objectively good at what they do, fail when working together as each finds the other person's way of delivering frustrating to deal with. Conversely, teams whose members are less effective on an individual level can achieve outstanding group results if they're sufficiently aligned. The take home point is that whether you're hiring or reassigning existing employees, ensuring alignment will de-risk your team building and set you up for success. With people-related issues at bay, you will have a team that works like a Swiss watch as well as more time and energy to focus on other topics.

Selecting for Alignment from the Start

Choosing the best "right" person means selecting someone whose work-related attributes are sufficiently aligned with yours and those of your team members.

Unfortunately, the best interview questions, non-verbal-cue-reading guru, and one-sided personality assessments will not help you assess interpersonal alignment. These Twentieth Century tools will never tell you what you critically need to know, namely whether you and your team will collaborate well with a candidate or not. It seems there is a better chance that we develop Superman's x-ray vision than the ability to assess alignment on the fly.

You will also never feedback someone into abandoning their (in their mind correct) perspective on these attributes and adopt yours. At best, employees can agree to follow processes regarding quality, timing, and communication, and acknowledging individuals who handle tasks particularly well may reinforce the behaviors you value.

Normally, insufficient interpersonal alignment leaves people, the manager and the managed, feeling wrong - for being too demanding or too sloppy or too something else. As a leader or as an employee, you know it's not fun to be on the receiving end of another person's judgment. Believe it or not, I have even worked with people who found fault with my military-minded working style.

Your Leadership Superpower

Selecting for solid interpersonal alignment from the start means you can let people be, including yourself. Instead of trying to cajole someone into being a certain type of person, more detail-oriented, more flexible, more timely, more motivated, selecting the people who resonate with your work style *naturally* will get you better results faster.

Ultimately, the only thing you'll ever have is what you give yourself. Come as you are. Accept that you don't have to change as a leader, be more charismatic, more inspiring, less demanding. And assemble a team whose members can be who they are, where each person's natural attunement is an asset and not a barrier to collaboration.

This isn't to say you can't strive to be better; everyone can work to be their best selves. But that can only happen when people are their true selves. The absence of personal criticism and judgment is exactly how individuals and teams thrive.

To put it another way, transformation doesn't come from following a prescribed list of things you need to change about yourself to become a great leader. Instead, it emerges from accepting that there is no hidden formula to being a great leader. As the great philosopher Kung Fu Panda put it so wisely, "There is no secret ingredient."

The Game-Changing Data You Need

Increasing your team collaboration requires you to know, based on data, not guesswork, individuals' interpersonal alignment. The only way to ensure a good fit is with a two-sided, bias-free approach. Meaning you need to understand both parties' compatibility, not one individual's personality traits. A good fit of work-related attributes between two people is the foundation of true connection, which in turn is the fertile ground for productive collaboration.

You can develop a method in-house or as stated before for assessing Values Alignment, leverage the platform OpenElevator has built to do just that. We deliver Interpersonal Alignment Data along with Values Alignment Data discussed in the previous chapter.

I'm very proud of the platform my team at OpenElevator has developed. I know it seems like a sales pitch, but I can't help but share my enthusiasm since I really believe in the platform we have developed. Using it, clients quickly get accurate answers to the following critical questions:

1. Who in the team naturally works well together and who does not?

2. Where are issues brewing and proactive support needed?

3. Who feels least connected within the team and is at risk of leaving?

4. Where can you improve collaboration and productivity?

5. Who are the best candidates to be promoted to team head?

6. Who if selected to team head would likely have high turnover?

7. Which top job applicants will collaborate best with you and your team?

8. Which top job applicants will not collaborate well with you and your team (and should not be hired)?

9. Which internal transfer candidates will collaborate best with you and your team?

10. Which internal transfer candidates will not collaborate well with you and your team (and should not be relocated)?

Team leaders immediately appreciate our method's validity because they see how spot on we nail their collaboration with each team member. They know from experience with whom they work smoothly, with whom it's a little more challenging, and with whom it's downright difficult.

Next, after validating the quality of their own collaboration with each person, our clients turn to see the rest of the team. For the first time, they have insight into how easily team members collaborate with each other (or don't). Remember, the scores reflect the two-person relationship, not a judgment of each individual: there are no good or bad people, no right or wrong coworkers.

It's the same for you. As a team leader, you already know the employees you work well with and the ones you can never seem to get through to. The data will not only instantly reflect your firsthand experience, but it will also help you maximize employee engagement and make decisions crucial to ensure your team's success.

Imagine how helpful it would be to know where the most productive collaborations lie and where things are not working so well between your team members. It's difficult to tell how well people will collaborate just by looking at them. They often go for lunch together; shouldn't they work well together? It's surprising how many cofounders use this "we're great friends" logic to start a company, just to learn how miserable it is to work together. And, in larger companies it gets more and more opaque to assess how well people are collaborating with every additional layer in an organization.

Seeing what the data reveals is powerful and empowering. Our clients immediately move from assuming to knowing their top performing teams. As one client put it, "it was so accurate *(it's almost scary)*. I got a few dopamine hits when I got the results." Once you see the data, you can't unsee it and knowing what to do becomes obvious. Some clients are made aware of issues brewing they hadn't suspected; others appreciate that the numbers reinforce what they'd already observed, giving them confidence to take needed measures. The actions clients take increases engagement and productivity.

In addition to upgrading collaboration in existing teams, leaders are able to leverage interpersonal alignment data in their hiring process. As I've noted, it is as important to understand how well candidates will work with you and your team as it is to know how well you and your existing team members work together. There's little point bringing someone on who will be difficult for you and your team to work with. It's no fun for them, either. Inevitably frustrated and disengaged, they'll likely soon resign, leaving you to redo the time consuming and energy draining hiring and training process all over again.

What I Have Learned from the Data

If you don't like your coworker, chances are your coworker doesn't like you either.

A person's gender, nationality, age, etc., won't tell you with whom they will mesh. Each person has their own innate working style and sees their way as the right way. I would love to believe that my structured, disciplined approach is the best way, but it's just the best way for me, not for everyone. The truth is, if you don't like working with someone, chances are they don't like working with you, either. (I'm looking at you Bonnie from procurement.) That's the magic of the two-sided assessment; it ensures that BOTH feel the ease of collaboration.

It's also not the case that everyone from Gen-whatever all love or hate one way of working. As much as two siblings are different, so are any two people in any given demographic group. The best (and only) way to identify people you will work well with is a two-sided, bias-free, data-driven approach. Without data, the quality of teamwork you'll get is just a toss of the dice.

Upgrading to Data-Driven Leadership

We have discussed the four drivers of long-term engagement: safety & certainty, contribution & purpose, growth & significance and connection & belonging. We emphasized that by getting to know, with data versus guesswork, how much safety & certainty, contribution & purpose and growth & significance each team member needs, leaders gain an edge, allowing them to define and implement a bespoke and powerful retention strategy to measurably reduce high employee turnover.

For the ultimate edge, leaders must go beyond these three drivers and address the most powerful driver of employee engagement: connection. Instead of wasting resources on the guaranteed-to-be-unreliable traditional methods, top interview questions, one-sided personality assessments, people with a self-proclaimed sixth sense, utilize data from our platform (or another source). This will save you and your organization time, money and the agony of working with the wrong people.

As I see it, you have three options. First, you can do absolutely nothing, stay exactly where you are right now, accept your current methods, flawed as they might be, and just deal with the costs on an on-going basis. Second, you can try a different recruiter, install a more rigorous job fit assessment, add additional interview rounds, include the latest personality tests and work through that entire process to find another employee who seems promising, then wait and see if collaboration and productivity improve. Or third, you can make a substantive change and give our platform a try – maybe on your smallest team or where you have the highest employee turnover – and see what results you get.

My goal is to give you practical, bias-free, data-driven insights to help you understand how well your current team members, or candidates, will work with each other and with the manager, ensuring their commitment for the long-term. The ultimate goal is to restore your time and resources, so you can navigate the sea more smoothly, successfully and even joyfully, to take your organization to new exciting destinations.

11

What Will You Do?

———

Do you know that it took close to two thousand years, from the time of Aristotle (circa 350 BC) until Galileo (circa 1600 AD) for it to be widely accepted that things fall at the same rate independent of their weight, even though that had already been demonstrated by others before Galileo?

This gives me hope.

Even if progress is slower than I would like, I'm very hopeful that we will move away from reliance on guesswork and gut feelings in our retention, relocation and recruitment processes and adopt data-driven, bias-free methods soon. I'm not sure if it's for you, but most leaders appreciate the value of data-driven decision-making. And considering it's possible to test-drive our assessment on a limited scope, a business area or a team, trying it is a no-brainer for most leaders.

Our clients, armed with our data-driven approach, are able to upgrade and de-risk their retention, relocation and recruitment processes. They get insights into where teams are working and delivering easily, where proactive intervention is needed, and where succession planning is in order. They can decide, based on data, whether retention strategies need an upgrade or if high turnover in a particular area is due to an interpersonal issue. Considering that each unwanted resignation costs an organization on average

$150,000, the investment of an assessment is negligible and the upside massive. You know very well measurably lowering your employee turnover permanently improves your bottom-line. It can also do wonders for your quality of life. Improved employee engagement is a win for all stakeholders.

Whatever you choose for yourself, your team and your organization, I wish you tremendous success.

www.ingramcontent.com/pod-product-compliance
Lightning Source LLC
Chambersburg PA
CBHW060336310726
48976CB00007B/2579